EVERYONE
REMAIN
CALM

EVERYONE REMAIN CALM

stories

megan stielstra

NORTHWESTERN UNIVERSITY PRESS

EVANSTON, ILLINOIS

Northwestern University Press
www.nupress.northwestern.edu

This is a work of fiction. Names, characters, places, and incidents either are the product
of the author's imagination or are used fictitiously, and any resemblance to actual persons,
living or dead, business establishments, events, or locales is entirely coincidental.

Printed in the United States of America

10 9 8 7 6 5 4 3 2 1

Library of Congress Cataloging-in-Publication Data

Names: Stielstra, Megan, author.
Title: Everyone remain calm : stories / Megan Stielstra.
Description: Evanston, Illinois : Northwestern University Press, 2021. |
    Originally published in 2011 by Joyland/ECW Press.
Identifiers: LCCN 2021026413 | ISBN 9780810143944 (paperback) |
    ISBN 9780810143951 (ebook)
Subjects: LCGFT: Short stories.
Classification: LCC PS3619.T53549 E94 2021 | DDC 813.6—dc23
LC record available at https://lccn.loc.gov/2021026413

For those of us who are never calm.

CONTENTS

Shot to the Lungs and No Breath Left

After Wade Dell Dallas put his fist in my eye on our third date, my father went after him with a .375 Holland and Holland Magnum.

Uncle Jack suggested that might be too much gun, seeing as the last thing it killed was a fourteen-hundred-pound bull moose. Every year, my dad and his brothers and all their sons—some fifteen beefy muscled Alaskan guys between the ages of six and sixty—loaded up two weeks' worth of gear and disappeared into the mountains, hunting moose. Or caribou. Or sheep, goat, elk—whatever had four legs to chase and a head to mount on the living room wall. I tried to imagine Wade's head up there next to the moose—his big ol' ears sticking out, the taxidermied skin wind-whipped and ice-burned raw, his stupid blue eyes blank and glassy. "Wade don't weigh more than one-eighty," Jack told my dad, who was squatted on the carpet loading up his field-pack. "That H&H'll spray his face straight backwards through his brain."

That's a pretty nasty image, especially for a fifteen-year-old girl in such a fragile emotional state, and my dad looked over to see if I'd lose it or something. What he saw was me on the couch, curled up in a ball with a pack of frozen peas over my left eye, the eye that two hours before had swallowed Wade's fist in a single gulp, knuckle bone on skull bone and everything went black. My dad turned to Jack then and said, "You see what he did to my girl?" His voice was quiet, the kind of calm that deep down points to crazy. "My one and only girl." He stuck a six-inch fixed-blade into his backpack. Then a GPS, a 10 × 40 spotting scope, and a meat saw. "Besides, I'm not gonna shoot him in the face," he said. "I'm gonna shoot him in the lungs."

In the Lower Forty-Eight, kids are taught not to run into moving traffic. Never talk to strangers. Ask before you pet the dog. In Alaska, we're taught to shoot for the lungs. "Here," Jack would say, pounding the meat between his chest and his armpit. "You aim here, for the lungs. A high shot'll hit the spine and a low shot'll hit the heart—either way, you're golden." My cousins and I hung on his every word: kill a moose, field-dress an elk, track a sheep, troll for salmon—we trained for the hunt the way other folks prep for the SATs, all my big boy cousins with their muscles and their rifles and their Suburbans and me, Shannon, the one lone little girl treading water in testosterone. I'll tell you what, though; they never treated me any different. I was one of the boys: gimme a knife, a gun, and twenty rounds of 300 grain soft points and I'll hold my god-damned own.

Dad'll say, "You see that?" pointing to the twelve-point caribou mounted over the sofa. "My Shanny whacked that bastard when she was eight years old, so don't give me none of that Girls Can't Do horseshit. My girl put a bullet right through that bastard's lungs!" Then he'd turn to me, his pigtailed daughter in size XS camouflage overalls with black paint smudged under her eyes to better blend into the brush. "Tell 'em, kiddo," he'd say—this is how we showed off, me and my dad—"Tell 'em how come the lungs."

I knew this script better than the Pledge of Allegiance. "When hit through the lungs," I'd recite, "a moose or game of similar size will bleed out through their muscles until the lungs collapse and the animal can no longer breathe." I'd seen this happen to every head up there on the living room wall and now—sitting on that couch with Wade's fist pounding in the back of my brain, the entire left side of my face numb from the peas, my dad loading bullets into waterproof baggies and my cousins all staring at me 'cause for the first time in our lives I wasn't one of them—I imagined what would happen to Wade when Dad's bullet slammed into the meat between his chest and his armpit.

It's a scene straight outta some Vin Diesel movie: that big, six-foot pretty-boy is hard at work at the petrol plant, loading Exxon barrels onto the back of some truck. Suddenly—a hard, fast whack to the chest, so fast he's not sure at first if it actually happened. He opens his mouth to speak but his breath is locked so he can't get out the words, just two hollow gulps of air before his lungs soak red like a wet sponge and slowly, slowly, blood seeps through the canvas of his coveralls. In one fatal, horrible second everything connects: The dark red-brown staining his chest. The airless gasping like some cancer patient with a cigarette. The punch above his heart like a shotgun with too much pull and then, after he's too empty of blood and air to keep on his feet, my dad walks right into his line of vision, that H&H Magnum pointed barrel to the ground. "Hey, there, Wade, how you doing?" he says, and Wade's stupid blue eyes go glassy and there's more blood on his uniform than there is in his body and in the last single second of life left in him my dad squats down and whispers: "She's my girl, Wade. My one and only girl."

My dad—he loves me like crazy. You can't hate that hard if you don't have love.

My cousins ran around helping Dad pack—flashlight, binoculars, plastic moose call, nylon rope—all trying their best to avoid my eyes 'cause, really, what would they do then? Say *Sorry*? Get me more peas? Pet my forehead the way a mom might've done?

One by one, the women in my family disappeared, sneaking down to California where water waved instead of froze and the sun shone the whole day. My dad and Jack and their brothers blamed the light—twenty hours of sun in the summer made you jumpy as a carton of Red Bull and twenty hours of dark in the winter was like living under a rock. "It takes some kinda woman to handle this life," they'd say, and my mother wasn't the kind they meant. One day I came home from elementary school and found her squatted on the sofa, talking to the caribou head. Another time, she bought me an Easy-Bake oven and all the guys—uncles and cousins and even my dad—started laughing. "What do you want Shanny to do with *that*?" he asked. "She's a killer, my girl!"

Not long after that she was gone.

All that happened ten years ago, and my dad still won't talk about it—just loads up his gear and heads to the mountains; trailing, tracking, searching for something, always something. That day he went after Wade, once they'd all took off and I sat alone in the living room, I tilted my head back and talked to those heads, the moose and the caribou and the big ol' curly-horned sheep. I said how I miss her. How I still have that toy oven, hidden in my closet under a box of tackle. How sometimes I hate being one of the guys, how I want to put on some of those fancy shoes they sell at Coles and go out to dinner, and that's why I liked Wade Dell Dallas and his stupid blue eyes and his *Hey, sweetheart* and his big, mechanic's hands—because he is the only man I've ever known who's made me feel pretty damn great about being a girl, even when the sonofabitch caught me right between the chest and the armpit, that shot to the lungs that stole the breath straight outta me.

Incredible

How it ended was, I got drunk. Like falling off the bar stool. Like lying on the floor and laughing at nothing. Like getting pulled to my feet by some random guy and falling over again, so he had to wrap his arms around my waist to keep me up. "Thanks," I slurred. And, "You're really ssstrong!" And, "You're cute, too. You got a ssshaved head, and a ssssweater, and that's a lot of sssss's."

So of course I took him home, and we were making out in the street in front of my apartment—pawing, groping, chasing each other up the stairs, kissing on the floor in the hall, and there we were at the front door, slobbering all over each other—good drunken anonymous fun that always makes sense at the time, and he said, "Should we go inside?" He had me pressed against the wall and I couldn't stop laughing. "We can't," I remember saying, sliding my hands down the back of his pants and nodding sideways toward the door. "He's in there."

"What?" the guy said, pulling back. "You live with your boyfriend?"

"Oh no," I said, still laughing. "There's no boyfriend anymore!"

"Well then, who?"

"You'll never guess," I said. "Guessss." I was really cracking myself up.

"Tell me," he said.

"Tell me," he said again.

"Tell me!" he insisted, so I said, singsong, "Okaaay. But you're just going to think I'm dru-unk."

He waited, and I leaned in close to his ear and whispered, "The Incredible Hulk lives under my bed."

He pulled away and looked at me, one eyebrow raised.

"I'm serious," I said. I squeezed his butt and tried to wink. "You wanna come see?" And then I was laughing and we fell through the door and clothes started flying as we stumbled down the hall: jacket, jacket, skirt, shirt, jeans, tights, all in our wake across my floor. I stopped in front of the bedroom and turned to face him in just my underwear. "Look," I said. "I haven't been in here in two weeks." I was trying to be serious but I had the whiskey giggles. "You see," I explained, "we had a fight."

This guy, he doubled over like that was the funniest thing in the god-damn universe. All he had on was socks, and I watched him laugh, and then I was laughing, but I also wanted to cry, and run, and touch him, and all these feelings bubbled, sixty-proof, in my stomach. "Just remember I warned you," I said, and then I opened the door.

It was dark in there, but enough moonlight was coming through the window to illuminate everything—silhouette of a dresser, outline of a closet, bed in the far corner, naked guy in socks. He tiptoed across the room and squatted down beside the bed. "Here?" he asked, rooting around beneath it.

Now, maybe it was the liquor, but I swear I heard music then, that *uh-oh, something's going to hap-pen* track, like in the movies when the pretty girl opens the basement door. "I'd get your hand outta there," I said. The music was getting louder, beating at the back of my skull. "Are you scared?" he said, and the music got louder, louder, and as I opened my mouth to tell him *Get back, just back away!* a long, thick, green hand shot out from under the bed, grabbed this guy around the ankle and yanked, his heavy, naked body disappearing in one smooth pull. The bed started shaking then like it was possessed, the blankets lifting up and falling down, the springs squeaking and groaning, the headboard slamming into the wall and there was yelling and growling and screeching, and then—just as suddenly—silence.

Maybe you're thinking I was just drunk. But it was for real. I swear.

How it started was my mother threw the television off the back porch. We were up on the fourth floor then, and I remember standing on my tiptoes to peek over the ledge and look down at the shattered TV on the pavement below. I don't know why she did it—I was five then and didn't understand their fights—but every time my dad came home with a new

TV, my mom would wait until he left the apartment, calmly unplug it, push it out the back door, onto the porch, and over the ledge. No yelling or threatening or retaliation worked, so my dad did the only thing he could—he hid one. When my mom would leave on Saturday mornings to go shopping, Dad would unlock the cabinet where he kept his hunting rifles, take out the secret television, twist aluminum foil around its rabbit ears, and we'd watch *The Incredible Hulk*. When David Banner would turn into the Hulk, his muscles all flexing and ripping through his clothes, my dad would roar and run around the living room pounding on his chest. He'd pick me up in the air and toss me all around, saying, "I'm that tough, aren't I, baby? I'm as tough as the Incredible Hulk!" He *loved* the Hulk, my dad, so much so that when he took off on Mom and me, he promised that I never had to worry, because "The Hulk'll take care of you, sweetheart. He'll always look after you." He was sitting on the edge of my bed as he said this. It was the middle of the night and from the light in the hall I could see suitcases packed and ready to go. I was six years old, and that was the last time I saw my father.

But true to his word, every time I had a problem the Hulk would appear. I got picked on in the schoolyard, and suddenly he was there, big and green in split red pants, picking up bullies and tossing them over jungle gyms. I took a really hard test, and there he was, squashed into the kiddie desk behind me, whispering answers over my shoulder. I got into a fight with my mom, and he'd be standing just behind her, sticking his green tongue out, doing the chicken dance with his fingers up his nose, anything he could to make me laugh. It was like I was some celebrity with a bodyguard, how he followed me around all the time, right up until I met Jerome my second year of high school. Jerome wore Birkenstocks and woven shirka parkas and beads made out of Fimo clay, so not long after I started dating him I wore flowy drawstring skirts and no deodorant. See, I was *love*. That's what Jerome said all the time: "Shelley, you are *love*. I don't just mean I love you, I mean, you *are* love," and I'd say, "Because of you." Jerome and me, we were all those things Shirley MacLaine talks about. I was going to meet him over and over again, life after life, all through the eternal wanderings of my soul, so you can imagine how I must've felt when he dumped me our first year of college. We were sitting across from one another at the Bali Café, drinking herbal tea, and he reached across the table and took both my hands between his own. His voice was very serious. "With you, I laugh, but not all of my laughter," he said. "I cry, but not all of my tears."

I said, "Huh?"

He said that institutionalized education was the displacement of the higher mind and he was going to Paris for real intellectual dialogue.

I said, "What?"

"I don't want any negative energy, Shelley," he said gravely. "What we had—"

Had?

"Was—"

Was?

"A real connection and—"

"I thought we were *love*," I said.

Jerome brought his hands together in Namaste and said, "I think we should just . . . be . . . *friends*."

I'll tell you what: I didn't feel much like *love* after that. I felt like bitter burning hatred, like sending anthrax to retirement homes, like giving machetes to babies, like pushing tourists off the Sears Tower observation deck and watching them fall like sinking stones through the atmosphere until they hit the pavement below and splattered grossness on everything in a ten-mile radius, that's how much I fucking felt like *love*! I ran back to my apartment, grabbed a pair of scissors, sat down in front of my mirror, and cut my hair off as I watched myself cry.

That was when I heard it—knocking from under my bed.

I sat perfectly still.

A few minutes passed, and then, again. Like knuckles on a doorframe.

"Hello?" I said. Nothing. I waited, then slowly stood up and walked to the edge of my bed. "Hello?" I said again.

Knock. Knock. Knock.

I stayed frozen for what felt like a long time, and then, slow-motion-slow, got on my hands and knees and lowered my head till my cheek was on the floor and I was staring underneath my bed.

Nothing.

And then, before I could stand up, there was a hand grasping my wrist and another hand locked around my ankle and I was yanked into the darkness beneath my bed, beneath his body, chest to chest with *I didn't know who*, his legs pinning mine down, one of his hands pressed over my mouth to muffle my screams and the other wrapped around my neck. We were eyeball to eyeball and I struggled under him, but it was too tight down there, he was too big, and the hand around my neck let loose and started moving down, over my chest, my stomach, down, down, his eyes still boring into mine and everything seemed to change all of a sudden, like the thermostat got turned up 'cause it was getting hot and when I realized what he wanted I stopped struggling against him and tried to help him get there: I lifted my hips up so he could get my jeans down, underwear off, all the time staring at him, and then he took his hand off my mouth and we were kissing and rolling and pressing and then I felt it—I gasped—and was blinded by a lightning flash of bright green light.

"You're *not* going to believe this," I said to my friend Celeste the next day at dinner. Her fork stayed suspended in midair during the whole story. "I couldn't really see anything," I said, "but I think he started out as Banner 'cause he just felt like a regular guy, you know, but after the green flash he just started growing. I mean . . . ." I dropped my eyes down to my lap and looked back up at her. "*Everywhere*. Like, I had my hands on his back and I could feel the muscles in his shoulders tighten and expand, could feel each ripple in his six-pack pop into place against my stomach. Like, suddenly he was three times as heavy so we had to flip over so I wouldn't be crushed and"—I whispered this last part—"his penis just inflated right up like he'd taken a bicycle pump to it! It was amazing!"

Celeste put down her fork and cleared her throat. "Shelley," she said. "Are you . . . doing okay?"

"Okay?" I said. "I'm fantastic!" I'd gone to a salon that morning and traded the clumpy chopped haircut for a little pixie cut, and had spent the afternoon giving my new Neiman Marcus card a workout.

"It's just that . . . I mean . . . sweetie," she said. "You're telling me you're in love with . . . the Incredible Hulk."

"I didn't say I was in love," I told her. "I said I got laid."

From then on I kept the Hulk to myself. I didn't tell anyone else about those nights with him under my bed, so there wasn't anybody to tell when they stopped. I just woke up one morning and he wasn't there anymore. That was the day I met Kyle, in a psychology class my junior year. A few months into our relationship we were making dinner at my apartment and he asked why all the artwork that I owned was still stacked on the floor.

"You've been living here forever," he pointed out. "Do you need help hanging this stuff?"

"No," I said. "I haven't decided on the right spot yet. Like, if I put the Bosch poster over here, above the fireplace, I'll want to switch it to the hall, and then . . ." I trailed off when I noticed the look on his face. "What's wrong?" I asked.

He sat me down on the couch next to him, reached over, and took both my hands between his own. "I've really enjoyed the time we've spent together," he said.

"You're talking in the past tense," I pointed out.

"I just think we're looking for different things."

"And what is it with guys grabbing your hands?" I said. "If a girl is going to drop a bomb in your lap she says, 'We need to have a talk,' but with guys it's grabbing your hands all the time."

"Shelley, I'm at the point in my life where I'm looking for a commitment," he went on, and was going to go on more but I cut him off.

"And I'm not?"

He let go of one of my hands in order to wave one of his at my paintings on the floor. "If you can't even commit to wall space you'll never be able to—"

I kicked him out. Then I found a hammer and banged the goddamn Bosch into the wall, lopsided. I went to my room and lay on the bed, on my back so the tears poured down the sides of my face and into my ears. That's when I felt it. A poke, like I had lain on a rock or something. I stayed very still and then, cautiously, I crossed one leg over the other and let it dangle just slightly over the edge of my bed. Nothing happened. I shook my foot a little. Nothing. I shook my whole leg, really rattled it around, like I was doing the hokey pokey. Nothing. *You're a fool, Shelley*, I said to myself, *it was a figment of your imagin*— but before I could finish the thought a green hand reached up, wrapped around my ankle, and pulled me down below.

For years, that's how it went. When I was with somebody, the Hulk was gone. When I wasn't, he was there. I mean, *really* there. There in your head as you fall asleep at night. There in your fingertips when you feel alone. There, after the others have all gone: the one who thought you were cold. Who thought you were fat. Who was a drunk. Who couldn't deal with your job. Who wanted to be with you but just *couldn't right now*. Who was *too busy*. Who was *not in a good place*. Who just *wasn't feeling it*. I'd look down at my fists clasped tightly between theirs and think that something incredible was a hell of a lot better than reality. In fact, I started rushing through breakups so I could hurry up and get under the bed.

"It's not you, Shelley," Carl said. I was twenty-five years old. He was Number Nine. We were sitting in his living room and—surprise!—he was holding both my hands.

"I think you're great," is what he said. "Really great."

"Okay," I said. "And?" My libido was revving, like somebody had just taken their foot off my brake.

"I really enjoy talking to you," he said, "and hanging out and stuff—"

"Right," I said. "And?"

"It's just that—"

Hurry up, man, spit it out!

"What I think I'm trying to say is—"

I don't have all night, I've got places to be.

"I think—"

No, I don't think you do, Carl. This is something you couldn't possibly understand.

"—Just . . . be . . . friends." he finished, and in a flash, I was on my feet. No beating of my breast, no ripping of my hair, no *why, why, why did it all go wrong?* No sir, I had places to be. I said, "OkaythanksCarlitwasfunbye," ran past his confused look and emotive hands, got out the door, into my car, and hit the streets at the corners, speeding all the way. See, I knew what would be waiting for me when I got home. It was always there—one, two, three, nine times—and I thought, *This is perfect! I'll never be hurt again, because the Incredible Hulk will always take care of me.*

11

But then something happened that I hadn't anticipated.

I fell in love.

I didn't mean to. I'd done everything I could to avoid it, dividing my time equally between work and Hulk. But there was, of course, the occasional night out with the girls, and that's when I met Jimmy. We were at a karaoke bar in Lincoln Square because Celeste needed to get a little Pat Benatar out of her system. While she sang, the rest of us drank, and cheered, and yelled for more, and by the time she got to "Love Is a Battlefield" the place was packed and everyone was hammered.

I pushed through the crowd toward the bathroom, slowly realizing how drunk I was by the effort of walking. I made it to the back and was going hand-over-hand down the wall when a voice behind me said, "You're not leaving, are you?"

Now, I know that everybody looks good when you've had a few, but when I turned around and saw this guy, I almost fell right over. He was beautiful. Beautiful. *But, Shelley, if you go back historically, so were Breakups Two, Five, and Six. And Five, Seven, and Nine were tall. Two through Five had good tattoos, and Three had soft thick hair and Four and Six had big brown eyes and Six, Seven, Eight, and . . . which one? Three, yes, and Three made you swoon when you first saw them, so . . . you see my point?*

"No," I said aloud. "I'm not leaving."

He smiled, and ohhhhh, the smile (*see Two and Five and Nine, please*), and said, "Good. 'Cause it's my turn pretty soon, and I'm dedicating a song to you."

I made it into the bathroom before I died, threw some water on my face, and looked at myself in the mirror. "No more," I said sternly to my reflection. I pointed my finger at me and tried to look threatening. "You said no more." Then I found my friends and said, "Come on. We gotta go."

"Are you kidding?" said Celeste. She had lipstick on her teeth and cigarette butts in her hair. "I'm just warming up!"

"Yeah, Shelley, what's your rush?" they all said, and I said, "'Cause *that* guy," and I pointed at the guy, the beautiful one, the one who would be Number Ten if we didn't get out of there quick, "is going to sing me a song."

This was excitement. This was information that can really ignite a table full of girls, and they immediately started taking bets as to what he would sing.

"John Hiatt, 'Have a Little Faith in Me,' " Liza said, and Celeste said, "Are you crazy? Look at that guy! He's not 'Have a Little Faith in Me'! He's 'I Wanna Fuck You Like an Animal'!" and Becky said, "You can't karaoke Nine Inch Nails!" and Celeste said she'd gladly prove the falsity of that statement, and Kelly said, "Ten bucks on 'Rocket Man,' " and everybody was like, "Elton *John*?" and money swapped hands and shots went all around the table and we were laughing and silly and suddenly, booming through the speakers came his voice, saying: "Okay, so . . . there's this girl."

"Yeeeah, Jim!" yelled one of his friends in the back.

"Shut up man," he said, and then he looked at me. "She knows who she is," he said, "and if I don't sing to her I'll regret it for the rest of my life."

Celeste poked me in the back then. That poke was girl-code for *Ohmygod did you hear what he just said? We all want them to say that.*

And then the music started. It was "The Joker" by the Steve Miller Band, and everyone in the room cheered, and sang along with "People call me the Space Cowboy, some call me the gangster of lo-ove, some people call me Maurice"—*Zooop zooop*—everybody always does the zoop zoop part—and who cared if this guy Jim had a good voice 'cause there was one stripe of hair falling across his eye and I thought *No more, I said no more*, and then I looked up and we locked eyes and the line was, "Don't you worry baby, 'cause I'm right here right here right here right here at home," and I was hooked. I'd like to pretend I'm tougher than that. That it takes more finesse to woo me, more time and thought into my seduction, but at that moment I felt like I'd been whacked over the head with a two-by-four. By the time he got to the "really love your peaches wanna shake your tree," I was ready. I would have followed him to the ends of the earth. The backseat of his car. Whatever.

When the song was done he came over to me.

He stood very close.

I remembered to breathe.

He opened his mouth to say something, but no words came, and he stared at me for a thousand million hours till finally he said, "So, I'm trashed, and I don't want to meet you like this so I was hoping we could get together tomorrow?" at which point Celeste poked me really hard and I knew they were listening, all of my drunk girlfriends splayed out behind my head like giant peacock feathers. "Definitely," I said, and he kissed me, fast, and then was gone, and when we all stumbled out of the bar that night singing *Zooop zooop*, I felt so good I thought I'd cry.

The next day was wonderful.

My favorite thing about it was there was another day after that which was equally as good, and after that there were more, and all those led to a single, perfect moment, sort of like how every river feeds the ocean. It'd been a couple months since we'd met and we were at the conservatory in that little outdoor garden in the back. It was one of the last warm days of fall and the sun was bright, us telling stories, us laughing, flowers everywhere all purple and perfect, and I kept thinking that word—*perfect perfect perfect*—and then there was a bee.

The thing of it is, I'm allergic to bees. I was stung once when I was five, and I puffed up bright red and kept swelling bigger till they sent me to the hospital. One of the few memories I have of my dad before he took off is him picking me up and driving straight to a friend's farm on the outskirts of the city. "I won't have you afraid," he'd said, and he took my hand and we walked right into the middle of a beehive—wooden frames with honeycombs in the middle set in circles across the lawn like a little Stonehenge—bees flying back and forth between them, around our heads, on our arms, in my hair, in my eyes like they might tangle in my lashes. I was still groggy from the drugs and very much associating these yellow and black bugs with all the needles they'd stuck in me. I opened my mouth to scream, but my dad crouched down in front of me, put his big hands on my shoulders and said, "Shhhhh. Be still, baby."

We stayed there like that, me and my dad, eye-to-eye, blue-to-blue, bees on our faces, light feather-touching across my skin, *Shhhhh, be still*, and I wasn't afraid.

But Jimmy, there in that garden? He was jumping all over the place, waving his arms to get the bee away from me. I put my hand on his chest, palm flat over his heart. "Shhhhh," I said. "Be still. It won't sting you if you're still." I felt his heart thump, felt that beat travel into my hand, down my arm, pounding through my body, and I knew I loved him.

14

I was sure.

That night, before I went to sleep, I sat down cross-legged on the floor next to my bed. With two fingers, I lifted the edge of the blanket so I could see underneath—there was dark. And dust bunnies. A book I'd been missing. One sock. Couple of stale crackers—and that was all. "Goodbye," I whispered, and, yeah, I felt a little silly doing it but we'd been together for so long that I felt I owed him at least that. "I'm glad you were there," I said. "But I don't need you anymore."

"We've got to talk."

Jimmy and I were sitting across from each other in some bar and out of the clear blue sky his hands were reaching over the table, snaking around the empty beer bottles and ashtrays and drink menus. My heart started to whack against the inside of my chest and I told myself *Shhhh, be still*, but nothing was and I wanted to throw things—the empty beer bottles and ashtrays and drink menus—just pick up everything I could and hurl it across the room. I wanted to cause some huge ruckus so everyone would turn and stare at us, and then he wouldn't be able to do it. The hands were still coming at me, and I locked my mine together and stuck them tightly between my thighs.

"Shelley," he said, and I couldn't breathe.

He said, "Look at me, will you?"

He said, "Come on." And out of my peripheral vision I saw his palms resting on the tabletop in front of me. "Come on," he said again. "Give me your hands." My stomach was sinking fast and I felt the tears, those stupid ones that you can't force back.

"No," I whispered. "I won't," and then it all burst out: "I won't give you my hands, Jim, because of that night we couldn't wait till we got inside so we made it on a couch someone had left in the alley. And I was looking for a pencil in your desk and found a list you'd made called Life's Goals, and number three was *Be a good dad*. And when we first got together you told me you wanted to take it slow and you're the first guy who's ever said that, who hasn't tried to get into my pants in the first fifteen seconds that we've known each other, and I am *not* ready for this to end!" With that, I stood up, grabbed an ashtray, and flung it across the room. It slammed smack into a neon Pabst sign, which shattered into a thousand glass shards all over the floor but was still plugged in and buzzing. That was the only sound in the room. Everything else was silent. Everyone in the bar was looking at me, and I felt so goddamn mad everything I saw was tinted red.

Actually: green.

A very *familiar* green.

I got home fast and burst into my bedroom, the door slamming into the wall and leaving hinge marks. "I know you're in here!" I yelled. I stood in front of my bed and stomped my feet. "I know you're supposed to save me, but I don't want it anymore! I want—" and that's when the hand shot out from under the bed, bright green against the white blankets, and locked around my right ankle. "No," I said, "not this time!" and I stepped down hard on his wrist with my free foot, really pounded on it, over and over till the bed started shaking and a muffled growling rose from beneath it. He pulled hard and my feet flew out from underneath me and I was on my back, dragged, watching as my body disappeared under the bed—first my feet, then my calves, my knees, thighs—I slammed both hands up against the sideboard and pushed back, trying to slide myself out—there were my thighs again, my knees, my calves—the growling was louder, louder still, the grip on my right foot iron-hard and groping for my left. I tried to remember the self-defense class I'd taken after Breakup Number Three and started kicking, aiming for where I knew his groin was, and, when I knew I wasn't hitting the mark, I flipped over onto my stomach and aimed my left foot at his face. That got results: my heel connected with his mouth, two hard kicks to the teeth and one more to the nose. He screamed then, lost his grip, and I crawled out from under the bed, arm-over-arm toward the door, and once I was all the way out I started to stand and that's when I heard it—the roar—the same one my dad had imitated Saturday morning again and again—loud and deep and raw and I turned and saw the hand, the wrist, the forearm, the elbow, the bicep, bulging, the shoulder, reaching out from under my bed, across the floor toward me. The electricity was going haywire, lights turning on and off, and suddenly everywhere there was noise—doors slamming and wind blowing and the bed dragging, dragging across the floor as he tried to get at me, lunging, roaring, screaming, almost on me, I couldn't move fast enough—he was there—no, I was free—no, he had me—my hand on the doorknob—his hand at my back—but I was through. I was out. I was slamming the door, sinking to the floor, covering my ears with my hands to block everything out.

I didn't go back into my bedroom for two weeks. I wore the same clothes. I had bruises on my legs from my fight with the Hulk and a huge purple welt on my hip from him pulling me to the floor. It hurt like hell and I slept on my side, on my couch, huddled into a ball at night listening to the sounds coming from behind that door—banging, roaring, tremors. What I heard during the day was no less disturbing: Jimmy on my voicemail.

"Shelley, are you all right?"

"Shell, what's going on?"

"You're freaking me out, Shell."

And finally: "It's been a week. I'm coming over."

I was sitting on the floor when I heard that one, backed up against the wall with my knees pulled into my chest. There was banging in my bedroom, Jimmy wanted to break up with me, was on his way over, I hadn't slept in a week, hadn't showered in longer, and I panicked. I did the only thing I could: went to the bar down the street and got drunk.

Brought someone home.

Took him to my bedroom

You know this part, I already told you. But what I didn't tell was that I woke up the next day, slumped in my underwear on the floor, and everything was normal. My bed was made. The door hung neatly on its hinges. No bruises. The only clothes on the floor were mine. Nothing was under the bed, or in the closet, or the pantry. Not in the cabinets. Not behind the couch. Not in any of the thousand places I could imagine something horrible—not in any corners fear could find. Everything was as it should be and my phone was flashing. I hit the voicemail button and got this: "It's me. It's Jim. I can't make you talk to me, but I need you to know that—"

I didn't hear the rest of that message, 'cause I'd picked my coat up off the floor, grabbed my keys, was out the door, into my car, hitting the streets at the corners, speeding all the way.

"Listen," I said, when Jimmy opened the door. He looked a little startled, and I tried to imagine how he was seeing me: barefoot, coat, no pants, hungover, hair wild, eyes wild, mind racing. "I know what you're thinking," I said, rushing through the words while I still had the courage to say them. "You think that I'm not good for you. You think you should leave. You think it won't work . . . but what I need you to know is, what's *really* there is so much different from what we *think*." I didn't know if I was saying it right, but I was trying, and that's more than I'd ever done before. "In the end," I said, "we think too much."

And you know what he did, this guy? He reached out and put one hand on my chest. "Shhhh," he said. "Be still." And I looked down and watched my heart pound into his palm.

The Boot

Penny got a collect call from the Illinois Department of Corrections and her imagination went a little crazy. What if it was Elliot, on a pay phone, fresh inky fingertips, using his one phone call?

Wishful thinking, she knew: Elliot was a law-abiding citizen. Elliot paid his taxes on time. Elliot looked forward to jury duty. Elliot, Elliot, Elliot. You know him, the guy behind the glass wall at the auto pound on Sacramento. He takes your VIN and your hundred-and-five dollars. He is stone-faced and cold, oblivious to sob stories or threats. "It's illegal," he recites, "to park or stand to obstruct a roadway less than eighteen inches of width on a two-way street or ten inches on a one-way street in accordance with the City of Chicago Department of Revenue." Elliot had always respected city departments and legal institutions in general, all except marriage, seeing as he'd left Penny—his soft, thick, pink-faced wife—left her without so much as a Dear John all alone in their tiny two-bedroom on the boulevard, watching anxiously out the front window.

After he'd been gone a week without word, Penny went to the auto pound to confront him. She rehearsed what she'd say on the drive down, trying out facial expressions in the rearview while waiting at red lights. Here is angry. Here is hurt. Here is dignified. She'd say this: "Elliot, how could you?" Her tone would be powerful, dramatic, very *NYPDBlue*. "You don't just leave. That's the coward's way out. It's spineless, and I deserve better." She tried out that last phrase a couple of different ways—*I* deserve better. I *deserve* better. I deserve *better*—and decided in the end to emphasize the I—I—me, this is about me, me standing up for myself, me fighting for what's mine. Penny felt empowered as she sped down

Sacramento—*forty* in a *thirty* zone, thank you very much!—and turned up Gloria Gaynor on the stereo.

The auto pound is a football field of barbed parking lot, gray and dismal, full of trapped, stacked cars and angry people waiting in line at the trailer office to present their registration, pay their fees, and bitch and moan. They don't want to pay the tow fee. They want to contest. It didn't say No Parking. The No Parking sign was behind a tree. The No Parking sign had graffiti on it. What do you mean, ten dollar per day storage fee? So if I got towed at midnight, that's an extra . . . what? What's expired? The line stretched back between the ropes, out the door, down the ramp, and into the parking lot. It was a slow-moving line and the closer Penny got to the front, the more she lost her nerve. She imagined Elliot looking up over his glasses at her, his shirt buttoned all the way up his neck. "Elliot, how could you—" she'd say as rehearsed, but he'd cut her off. "Vehicle identification?" he'd ask, as if she was any old person waiting in line, not his wife of five years whom he'd abandoned without warning! and she'd be so stunned that she'd forget her speech. "Vehicle identification!" he'd repeat, loudly, like she was deaf, and she'd stammer and eventually cry.

None of that happened, though, because Elliot wasn't there. It was a woman behind the glass partition, and her hair was dyed red like a candy apple. "Vehicle identification?" she said. She didn't look up at Penny as she spoke, just held her hand toward the hole in the wall, waiting for the appropriate paperwork to be slid through. Her nails were red acrylic and she wore cheap gold rings on every finger. Penny knocked timidly on the glass to get her attention. "May I speak with Elliot, please?" she asked.

The woman raised her eyebrows. They matched her hair. "Who are you?" she asked.

Penny hesitated. "His wife," she said.

The eyebrows went higher. Penny was suddenly afraid of what this woman knew about her. Maybe she was Elliot's confidant and had listened to him talk about how he and his wife were growing apart. How she had put on weight over the past couple years. How he didn't come to bed till after she'd gone to sleep, and if she tried to touch him, he took his pillow and went to the couch, and one night she'd gotten desperate and had put on some godawful lacy underwear and tried to—she just tried too hard.

20

"He transferred to another office," the woman said.

Penny couldn't speak.

"Will you hurry up?" snapped someone behind her. "I'm getting old just—"

Her eyes were tearing up. She didn't know what to do with her pride.

"Come on!" came the voice behind her, and another voice said, "Goddammit, lady!" and lots of other voices started to grumble and rise, and the redhead stood up behind the glass wall. "You're going to have to step asi—"

"Where is he?" Penny asked. Her voice was small and scared. She wanted to melt and trickle toward the door.

"What did you say?" asked the redhead, loudly, annoyed, "I can't hear—"

"I said, where is he?" Penny found a spare ball of strength hidden away in the corner of her stomach and looked the woman in the eye. One-Mississippi. Two-Mississippi. Three-Mississippi.

"I'm sorry," the redhead finally said. "Do you have photo identification?"

Penny imagined breaking down the glass and getting that woman in a chokehold across the counter. "You tell me where my husband is, you Crayola-haired bitch," she'd hiss, and would grasp hold of one long, sculpted nail between two fingers and bend it precariously back. "I don't know," the redhead would gasp from the limited air in her windpipe. A snap—a shriek—one nail down, four to go—"I asked you a question!" "I told you I don't"—*snap*—"know!"—*snap*—"Goddamn!"—*snap, snap*—"Still got five more, sweetheart!"—bending, bending, almost there—"Okay okay *okay!*" The woman'd write down an address with her one working hand and Penny would loosen her grip. She'd look up and see the miles and miles of people waiting in line to get their cars—all of them staring at her, mouths open, eyes pleading—and feel an overwhelming sense of purpose. She'd rush to the gate and throw it open. "Run, my friends!" she'd cry, as swarms of humankind ran to the lot and toward their vehicles. "Go! Be free! Drive home to your wives!"

That was the fantasy.

This was the reality: Penny, in a baggy dress and too much eye makeup, pressing her palms against the glass dividing wall. Never before had she felt this low. She was begging a woman with fake red hair to tell her about her very own husband. "Please," she implored, humbly, simply. Pride was gone, only hope left. "Please."

The woman looked down at her paperwork.

There went the hope.

It came back on the day the Department of Corrections called. Penny accepted the charges and imagined Elliot in prison. She knew what it was like in prison. She watched *Oz*.

It wasn't him, though. It was a mechanical-sounding voice telling her that the conversation would be recorded. Then a fuzzy joggly sound. Then a man who thought she was someone else.

"Michelle?" said the man.

"No," said Penny. She'd wanted it to be Elliot. It'd be a lot easier to deal with him being taken away that it was with him leaving on his own.

"Michelle there?" the man asked.

"There's no Michelle here," she said.

"Yes, she lives there," he said. "She told me she did."

"I'm sorry," said Penny.

"Come on, lady. I know she's there," he said.

Penny hung up. She didn't want to deal with someone else's needs. She had too many of her own.

The Department of Corrections called many times over the next few months, but Penny never accepted the charges. She went about her daily business—operator for AAA, cleaning the apartment, cable television—but always listening for the sound of Elliot's car, checking the answering machine, the post office, the mailbox, the inbox: nothing. Still she waited—waited and waited and waited—until something finally happened.

Penny got a parking ticket. Her first ever. She'd stopped at Kmart to pick up some of those Pledge Grab-It dusters that she had a coupon for, and had inadvertently parked outside the diagonal markings. Code 09-64-030(b). Twenty-five-dollar fine. Twenty-one days till it doubled. She could hear Elliot's voice in the back of her head: "It's illegal. Illegal. Illegal."

Penny set the parking ticket in the center of the dining room table, poured herself a glass of wine, and sat down to consider her options.

What should she do with it? The logical answer, of course, was to pay it. But Penny was a little bit angry with logic. Logic hadn't been good to her lately, why should she be good to it? She glared at the parking ticket. It made her think of Elliot: *you have broken the law*, it seemed to say, like on her birthday when he'd refused to dance with her in Buckingham Fountain. "We can't," he'd said, holding her arm. She'd toed off her shoes and implored him to live a little. "You're drunk," he'd said, and she'd said, "It's romantic," and he'd said, "It's illegal."

Penny took the ticket to her bedroom and went to the closet. From the top shelf she pulled a carved wooden box that she'd bought on their honeymoon in Santa Fe. She kept things that Elliot had given her over the years: origami birds he folded out of deli receipts, first-second-third-fourth anniversary presents, a stack of letters he'd written when they'd first met and had gone to different colleges in different states. She'd meant to put the ticket in the box, as if her parking outside the diagonal lines was another milestone in their relationship, but instead put the box on the floor and sat next to it, legs crossed, back against the bed. She took one of the letters out of its envelope, read the *Dear Penelope* at the top, and got up again. A few minutes later she returned with the wine, sat back down in the same place, and continued reading.

Here are some of the sentences: *I think of you often. We are fortunate to have met each other. I've been considering our future.*

There were others, but they all read the same: tepid, at best. Penny wondered how she ever thought he loved her. By the time she'd finished all the letters, the bottle was gone, too, and Penny cried for all the things he was supposed to have said but hadn't. *I love you* and *I need you* and *sweetheart* and *darling*, and before she knew it she was ripping the letters into little pieces, slowly at first, with deliberate, even strips; then angry and destructive, papers flying around the bedroom, origami birds crunched underfoot, deep gutsy sobs pulling from her middle till she finally collapsed in a lump and balled into the carpeting, that sniveling pathetic sort of crying, the soundtrack to desperate acts.

The phone rang then. Penny reached up to the bedside table, fell over, picked herself back up, and let the receiver topple to her lap. "This is a collect call from the Illinois Department of Corrections," said the mechanical voice. "Will you accept the charges?"

She most certainly will.

"Michelle," he said, after a beat or two. "Baby, is that you?"

Penny bit back a wail. *Baby, is that you?* Why hadn't anyone ever said that to her?

"Baby?" he said again, "Baby, I'm dying in here," and Penny realized that she'd have to say something back. She felt fuzzy, like she might faint, and all she wanted to do was curl up around the phone and hear him say *baby* until she fell asleep. She sniffled loudly, and made some of those gaspy sounds like when you're trying to get your crying under control.

"Shhhh," he said. "I know."

The room swirled now. "You do?" she asked, through the phlegm and salt.

"I do," he said. His voice was sad, and sensitive, and deep. Penny shut her eyes and imagined the man that wrapped around that voice. Strong arms, and a thick chest to lean against, and stubble, and eyes with very dark lashes. "I know how hard it is," he said.

He knows, Penny thought through the haze.

"Just remember that I love you," he said, then the automated switch, then static, then the dial tone. Penny sat there on the floor, the phone pressed against her ear, listening to the silence where he'd once been.

The letter came a week later. It had Penny's address and Michelle's name typed on the front, and on the back was a blue stamp that read THIS CORRESPONDENCE IS FROM AN INMATE OF THE ILLINOIS DEPARTMENT OF CORRECTIONS. Penny stood at her mailbox for a long time, looking at that envelope. Then she brought it inside, set it down in the middle of the dining room table, and looked at it some more.

Here is what she *should* do: write *Return to Sender* on it and put it back in the mailbox.

Here is what she *wanted* to do: open it, read it, memorize it, sleep with it, read it again, read it eighteen thousand times, and develop an elaborate fantasy.

Here is what she *did* do: sprint down the hall, rush to the closet, pull down the Elliot box, close the letter into it, put it back on the shelf, slam the closet door and lean against it, breathing heavily.

This was how Penny always dealt with desire: ignored it, hid from it, denied it. Last year she'd tried one of those diets where you couldn't eat any complex carbohydrates, and, almost immediately, bagels started talking to her. *Eat me*, they'd say, *just this once*, and after a while the noodles joined in, and the crackers and rice, too. Penny had to run around the kitchen with a Hefty Cinch Sak, sweeping all the offenders into it and throwing them to the curb.

She would *not* give in to desire. Desire was dangerous. She would be safe.

For a while anyhow, because more letters arrived—five, ten, twenty showing up in the mailbox. Penny put them all in the closet and closed the door, hoping to forget about them, but temptation is a strong drug. Every time she went into the room the closet would rattle. They wanted to be opened. She'd shut her eyes and try to calm the beating in her chest—no go. The more letters Michelle received, the more the closet shook. Penny remembered *Poltergeist* and got paranoid. She avoided the bedroom, keeping the same clothes on for days at a time and sleeping on the couch. She fought a great inner battle: *Open it! No! Yes! Shut-up shut-up shut-up!* The more letters she put in the box, the louder the yelling in her head till eventually she decided *Enough is enough* and let the envelopes stack up in the mailbox. She took to driving mindlessly around the city, putting distance between herself and Pandora's box. She'd stay away for hours, camping out in bookstores and wandering the aisles of grocery stores. There were dark circles under her eyes and she was *thiiiiis* close to losing her cookies.

That's when it happened: the parking ticket. This one was 09-64-100(g). Parking within thirty inches of a traffic signal. "Goddammit!" she yelled, grabbing the orange envelope. "Why can't you leave me alone!" She ripped furiously, dropping her purse to the ground to get at it with both hands, taking the small pieces and shredding them even smaller till there was nothing left and then she stopped. She stood there, on the sidewalk, breathing heavily, and realized—as the wind picked up the orange scraps and spun them in the air—that she felt good. So good, in fact, that the next day she parked within fifteen inches of a fire hydrant while she ran into the Currency Exchange. When she saw the familiar orange underneath the windshield wipers, she felt a great rush. "A hundred dollars, eh?" she said, as she grabbed up the ticket. "This is what I think of your hundred dollars, Elliot!" and the confetti hit the wind. The next morning, it was street cleaning. Penny drove around looking for the signs attached to trees, and parked wherever she saw them. One, two, three, four tickets by 3:00 p.m., a grand total of two hundred dollars sailing to the sky, and Penny was giddy. The day after that it was loading zones, and then underpasses, and then disabled parking in public and private lots, and she felt wild and reckless and drove right up onto the sidewalk in front of 7-Eleven as she ran in for a Slurpee. When she came out: the boot.

Penny stared at it, the metal cage locked around her back driver's side tire. Then she laughed. Then she walked into the nearest bar and sat there for the next four hours drinking Maker's Mark until somebody put her in a cab. She teeter-tottered into the house, made for the closet, and read every damn letter he'd sent.

This time the temperature was *just* right: boiling burning scalding hot. All the necessary words were present and accounted for: *love, cherish, desperate, desire,* and *Henry.* His name. *Henry.* Henry loved her and cherished her and was desperate with desire and didn't know if he could go on sitting in that jail cell going crazy from Not Knowing where she was and what she was doing and if she was still his or not and in her wild, drunken, wobbly hand she wrote *I Love You* on the back of a picture postcard, took it through the midnight darkness to the mailbox, and made it back inside before she passed out.

So it began.

Penny and Henry wrote every day. Theirs were long, soul-searching letters. Henry asked for forgiveness: *I'm making good in the eyes of society, babe,* he wrote, *but what am I in your eyes?* Penny wept over his words. When she found out what he was asking forgiveness *for,* she used it as yet another piece of evidence that they were destined. Henry in prison for grand theft auto? A coincidence? I think not! Penny was smart enough not to laugh in the face of fate, and this—*this*—was fate. She was in love and you could see it. She had that glow that they talk about, lit up like a saint as she walked, and since her car had been impounded, she walked everywhere. With the walking came the weight loss, and with the weight loss came the new clothes, and the confidence, the love of life, of her fellow man, of herself, and everything was wonderful and beautiful and perfect.

Except for one thing: she wasn't Michelle, but she could've managed to ignore *that* fact if it hadn't've been for *this* one: Henry wanted to see her. He wrote it at the end of every letter.

Eventually there were more letters than there were excuses.

The visit room was crowded with couples and families reuniting. In the middle of all of them, Penny sat alone at a metal table, staring at her hands in her lap and waiting. She had on a new dress from Marshall Field's. Size eight. She'd gotten a makeover that same morning at the Mac counter, and there was perfume, too—Dior—and a manicure. She figured the only way to kill Henry's shock at her not being Michelle was to be better than Michelle, so there she was—better—the best. She had never looked so good. Amazing, what love will do to a girl: you start to see yourself the way he sees you, and Henry, Henry loved her.

Didn't he?

A couple of guys had just walked into the visit room, all wearing denim and looking around for their mothers/girlfriends/wives/children. Was he there? Penny inhaled sharply and looked back at her hands. She shouldn't be here, shouldn't have signed Michelle's name on the prison visitor log, shouldn't have pretended to be someone she wasn't. *This was a horrible, horrible mistake*, she thought, and started to stand up.

That was when she felt it.

The look. That at-you, in-you, through-you look. Penny lifted her head slowly and—there. He was leaning against the wall at the far end of the room and everyone else suddenly vanished. He was big and burly and beautiful, and their eyes locked, and she knew it was him.

"Hey," came a voice at her elbow. She glanced up quickly and saw a wispy little guy wearing the same denim shirt. "Hello," she said, being polite, and then turned back to Henry, her hair spinning almost slow motion, like a shampoo commercial.

"Okay if I sit here?" the little guy asked, indicating the empty chairs at the table. "I'm waiting for my girlfriend."

"Whatever," said Penny, not really listening, too involved in this first seduction. Henry's eyes were all over her body, traveling up her feet, legs, stomach, chest, neck, mouth, and back on down, a wave of warmth. She was acutely aware of heaving. She hadn't ever heaved before.

"She must be running late," said the little guy, sitting down across from her. "Her car got impounded."

"Oh," said Penny. Every second Henry didn't touch her was agony and the anticipation mounted, but something about drawing this moment out was strangely intoxicating—

"She'll be here, though," said the little guy. His face was a bit pockmarked.

"Uh-huh," Penny said, completely oblivious to everything but Henry. She wanted him to grab her, maybe a little too rough, but how rough was too rough when—

"I'm kind of nervous. I haven't seen her in a really long time," the little guy was going on. Penny turned to face him and shot him a very calculated look, the same one you give to the guy who won't stop talking when you're trying to read. Then back to Henry, back to heaving.

"Are you waiting for someone?" asked the little guy.

"Yes," she said. *I'm waiting for that hunkrock leaning against the wall and I'm going to go over there and climb him like a tree.*

"That's good," said the little guy. "I mean, it's so nice that you came. We get to wondering in here. Like with Michelle—that's my girlfriend— it sucked for a while 'cause I—"

For a single moment, all motion stopped, like the pause button on her life had been hit. Penny found herself being pulled by two very strong opposite forces. She turned and looked at the little guy. Then she turned and looked at the beefcake. Back and forth, back and forth, and then time started again.

"—didn't know if she still loved me, you know?" Henry was saying. "So I'm just saying, be sure to tell him," he finished, and smiled a big, toothy grin.

Penny smiled back. "I will," she said, and then she leaned across the table and took Henry's hands between hers. "Thank you," she said, and stood up. She walked out of the room, feeling both men's eyes at her back. Then she retraced her steps to the bus stop and sat, waiting to drive off to the next thing.

Times Are Tough All Over

Paulie hangs out in the parking lot at Target, waiting for the mothers. The newer the better. They're easy to spot: hair a mess, eyes hazy from lack of sleep, shopping carts stuffed with diapers and formula that they leave outside the car as they pack their babies into car seats. That's when Paulie makes his move—grab the cart and run. Not like she's going to catch him, right? You can't leave your kid behind. Paulie knows this. He's got a kid at home, too.

Bernadette attends house meetings for Organizing for America. She's never voted in her life and doesn't plan to start, but they've always got snacks. When no one's looking, she pockets the leftover mini sandwiches; saves five bucks the next day at the cafeteria. One time, she got away with *six* sandwiches—six times five bucks is a lot of money. You can do a lot with that kind of money.

Jean can't afford the movies. Three kids at $12 a ticket? Plus popcorn?—forget it. So what she does is pop some Orville Redenbacher in the microwave, load everybody in the car, and drive to stuff that's cool: a lightning storm over Lake Michigan, that house on Humboldt Boulevard with the crazy Christmas lights. They sit there, in the dark, passing the popcorn, watching.

Rebecca's husband travels a lot, so she got a cat. It looked like the one eating from crystal goblets on TV commercials: long silky orange hair. Within the week, there was long silky orange hair all over Rebecca's white formal living room; white carpet, white chaise, white marble, white drapes, white throws. Rebecca considered redoing the living room again, something that wouldn't show the hair. Something orangeish. What are they calling orange these days? Sienna? She even went through the Rolodex and found her designer's cell number: it would be fun; it would kill time; fill up the hours passing so long, so slow, molasses through a sieve. In the end, she decided against it. Another room design wasn't practical, not in today's economy. She put the cat in the carrier, drove to Animal Cruelty, and asked if she could trade it for a white one.

After Andy's dad got laid off from GM, Andy went to the Hyundai lot in the middle of the night. So, okay: he'd had a few. Fine: more than a few. He'd fucked up the ACTs, his dad was on the couch, what else you going to do? "All the shiny fucking new Jap cars in their perfect fucking rows." He flipped open his Zippo and leaned over the gas tank. "Fucking Hyundai. Fuckers." It made sense at the time.

What Lou does is this: after the customer gives him the credit card receipt, he adds an extra number to the tip. Like, if they left five bucks, he puts a one in front of the five and gets paid out fifteen. See? A 3 in front of a 9 is 39, and 39 bucks is half his gas bill. Half his gas bill on one table. Nobody's come after him yet, so he's getting greedy; last night he added a one in front of the twelve. Hundred and twelve bucks. Hundred and twelve. Shit. It's almost worth getting caught.

Delia took off her clothes. She'd said she'd never do that.

All these kids graduating from college. There aren't any jobs. So they go for more college—things'll turn around by the time they finish the second time.

Marcus heard a story about a guy who made money on the internet. Six figures in the first year! He didn't know much about computers, but it would be easy to figure out, right? Anybody can build a website. There were all those free tutorials! Free ebooks! Free webinars! Free once you signed up for a monthly subscription! Free with your credit card number! Free with your email address! FREE! EVERYTHING'S FREE!

Abby's dad slammed the door so hard the hinges cracked and her mom yelled *those* words at his disappearing back. Then her mom leaned on the counter and cried. Then she remembered Abby was there and gave her a hug. "You have to kiss lots of frogs before you find your prince," she said into Abby's hair. She'd said that a lot, so today, wearing her astronaut costume, Abby went to the creek behind the house with a bucket. She caught seventeen frogs, the highest number she could count, and then sat on the back porch kissing them. The first few were slimy and gross, but, after a while, their skin dried out in the bucket and it felt like eating sand.

What can you sell? Look around your living room—do you really need all that *stuff*? Books, CDs, DVDs; the shelves from IKEA; that coffee table from your grandmother; the plants—plants are expensive, somebody'll buy the plants; those are nice fixtures, too; you'd be amazed at what pipes cost; even the nails are worth something these days. Everybody needs nails.

Deb sold blood. Frank sold sperm. Eliza sold jewelry. Wally sold his hair. Kristine sold her eggs. She was an excellent candidate, they told her at the clinic—white, blonde, with a graduate degree. She could charge top dollar.

Alex sold urine. It was a niche market. He had a cushy, door-to-door job with a health insurance company: he'd go to the homes of potential clients, give them a special plastic cup, and wait while they peed. While he waited, he'd look at their stuff—their books, their art, their music. If they took a while—sometimes people take a while— he'd go through their drawers. One time, he found the glass pipe, the old olive jar packed with pot. On the table was a half-drunk gallon of cranberry juice—*Slick*, Alex thought. No way was this guy's pee clean, no way would the insurance company sign him, and when the guy came out of the bathroom, Alex made him an offer. He had a case full of urine. He had a daughter in private school.

> When we were kids, we collected empty pop cans out of the trash and returned them at ten cents per; fifty cans'd fill your gas tank. We are grown-ups now, and we still collect those pop cans. Takes a lot more of them, though.

It wasn't Tim's fault. First he had the flu. Then the bookstore sold out of the textbook. Then his friend moved to Florida so he had to help—Tim *explained* all this to his physics professor. He'd *done* the homework! He *knew* the material! He *had* to pass the class, he just *had* to, any more withdrawals and they'd kick him out of the dorm—just *one more* extension—and the day *that* rolled around— you won't fuckin' believe it—his hard drive exploded! It just, like, exploded! What was he supposed to do? He couldn't fail this class, not *again*, so what he did was call the college's main line. He told them he'd seen a bomb. He got the idea from some Denzel Washington movie: everybody evacuates, classes are canceled, and he gets one more week. He just needs one more week. Except on the phone? They asked who was calling. Tim panicked. He used the name of some visiting lecturer he'd seen in the school paper. Some Muslim guy. Everybody gets all worked up about the Muslims, I mean, *he* doesn't, *Tim* doesn't, *Tim* is fine with the Muslims, he's not *like that*—but what else was he supposed to do?

> First the husband lost his job. Then the wife. They put their condo on the market, but nobody's buying, nobody's buying, nobody's buying. Even now, as you read this, nobody's buying.

On People.com, there's an actress who had to sell one of her houses 'cause she couldn't afford three separate mortgages. Times are tough all over.

> Rent, groceries, gas, childcare, bills. Which don't you pay?

First, ice the bruise to reduce swelling. You can use a bag of frozen vegetables; peas or carrots. Next, a yellow-green shade of eye shadow. Green offsets the red; yellow hides the blue. Apply from the center out. Let it dry—you might need another application. Next, foundation the same tone as your skin. Finally, setting powder. Joanne practiced in the bathroom mirror. She'd been planning on leaving him, but yesterday she got a pink slip. So.

> There's this self-help doctor who suggests we all go on news fasts; no reading about the world in order to improve our worldview. Is this the dumbest thing we could ever do, or the smartest?

Lisa is having a hard time concentrating in yoga class. She'll be doing her breathing, doing her Pigeon, her Warrior III and her Upward Facing Dog, and then her mind will wander to all the things she's taking a yoga class *not* to think about. To help, her instructor gave her a mantra: *netti netti netti*. It means *not that*. When bad thoughts come to her, she's supposed to think *netti netti netti*; *not that not that please not that*.

What to do with the frustration? Where do we put it? Some go to therapy, some drink, some bitch about politics, some yell at NFL refs, some make art, some pray, some volunteer, some enlist, some plant a garden, some have another baby, some play video games, some take seminars, some sleep too much or not at all, some eat too much or not at all, some count to ten. Nine. Eight. Seven. Six. Five. Four. Three. Two. One.

Nick drives a bus, and every time he sees somebody running from the other side of the street, waving their arms yelling *wait wait wait!* he hits the brakes and sits there till they arrive. Sometimes, people already on the bus get pissed. They have places to be, they're running late, another bus'll be here in a sec! But Nick just sits there. There are so many things in his life he can't control; but this? Waiting for that guy or girl or kid or whoever running down the street?—that's all him. That's something he can do, one little thing in the middle of a shitstorm and goddammit, he'll wait. He'll wait all goddamn day.

Professional Development

You must live in the present, launch yourself on every wave, find your eternity in each moment.

—HENRY DAVID THOREAU

He lay sprawled, too wicked to move, spewed up like a broken spider-crab on the tarry shingle of morning. The light did him harm, but not as much as looking at things did; he resolved, having done it once, never to move his eyeballs again. A dusty thudding in his head made the scene before him beat like a pulse. His mouth had been used as a latrine by some small creature of the night, and then as its mausoleum. During the night, too, he'd somehow been on a cross-country run and then been expertly beaten up by secret police. He felt bad.

—KINGSLEY AMIS

Every year I attend the national AWP conference. AWP stands for Association of Writers & Writing Programs, an umbrella organization for writers, teachers, and publishers across the country. For five days everyone comes together for scholarly presentations and panel discussions with such titles as "Judy Blume: The Challenges and Pleasures of Writing about Teenage Girls" or "To Censor or Not to Censor: The F-Word in the Classroom." So, picture it: thousands of writers taking over convention centers in Kentucky, Baltimore, Chicago, and—this particular year—New Orleans.

I flew in late Tuesday night and took a cab to my hotel. It was in the French Quarter, which, for me, was a dream, someplace you read about in an eighteenth-century novel: the Spanish architecture, the elaborate iron balconies, the colored walls and hanging vines and lights and music and laughing, smiling people. So many happy people—it couldn't possibly be real.

I was sharing a room with my colleague, Abe, who'd arrived a day earlier. Abe taught service-learning classes, believed fundamentally that good teachers can change the world, and wore very tight jeans. "Hurry up," he said. He was in front of the mirror, fixing the barely perceptible Mohawk in his perfect hair. "We're going to the Dragon's Den, and after that—"

"It's nearly midnight," I told him, sitting down with the AWP schedule. Just out of grad school, it was my first year teaching and my first time at the conference. I had a lot to learn and more to prove. "We've got to be up at seven for Non-Gender-Specific Pronouns in Erotic Poetry."

Abe turned and looked at me. "We're in New *Orleans*," he said.

"We're at AWP," I corrected. "Remember? Professional development?"

"But you don't even write poetry! Let alone erotic poetry, I mean, when was the last time you even got laid?"

Okay, so I work a lot.

I know that everybody works a lot, but I work a lot in the way that my therapist calls an "avoidance mechanism." As in, I'm fairly screwed-up but I don't have the time to do anything about said screwed-upedness because I'm too busy at work. "Nothing a little fun won't cure!" Dan says—Dan is the guy I have dinner with occasionally but it won't go any farther 'cause I'm too busy at work—and I say, "Fun isn't part of my five-year plan."

Abe sat on the edge of my bed with a very serious face. The kind of face one might wear during an intervention. Me, I don't drink much. Half a glass of wine and I'm out to lunch. "Megan," he said, "you need to have some fun."

"I need to go to bed."

I attended seven panels Day One of AWP: eight to ten, ten to eleven-thirty, noon to one-thirty, one-thirty to three, three to five, five to seven, and seven-thirty to nine.

"You're in New Orleans and you spend thirteen hours in a conference hall?" Abe said that night. He was preparing to go out. I was in bed, preparing for tomorrow's retrospective on Women Writers of the Late 1800s.

The next night, when I got back to the hotel, there was a voicemail message from the chair of the Fiction Writing Department, my boss. "Megan," it said. "I order you to get out of that hotel room. Meet us downstairs at ten; we're going dancing." I pushed delete and practiced my lie in front of the mirror: "Why no, I never got that message!" I said, in my best *Oh my, officer, am I speeding?* voice, one I'd started with my therapist and perfected with Dan. Like *Of course I want to see you, I just can't tonight!* or *Of course I'm telling you the whole story, I don't have anything to hide!* or *Oh, rats! Dancing! I love dancing!*

The truth is, I'm afraid—but at that point, I hadn't admitted it. Is there ever a point where we admit it? It's easier to live for our work. For our books. For tomorrow's panel on *Finnegans Wake*.

I spent Day Three of AWP in similar dorkishness, and would've done the same Day Four had I not got a phone call at 3:00 a.m. "Get your ass up. Get in a cab," Abe yelled over the music—more like slurred. *Yell-slurred.* "And get a pen, I'm giving you an address."

"Do you know what time it is?" I said.

"It's called the Funky Butt," he said.

I hung up.

He called right back. I hung up again, and, again, he called back. This time—instead of being all drunk and stupid—he said, "What would Henry say?"

Okay. So, when I was really little, like seven or eight, my dad was writing his graduate thesis on Henry David Thoreau. He's really *into* Thoreau. He has exactly three chairs in his house: "One for solitude, two for friendship, three for society." When I got my first tattoo, he said, "What would Henry say?" *And*—you know those leather book covers for your Bible? They say BIBLE in all caps across the front? My dad had one of those around his copy of *Walden*. You see where this is going, right? I spent the first eight years of my life thinking *Walden* was the Book of God. I even had to memorize passages! Picture it: Daddy's Little Girl in her OshKosh

B'gosh and pigtails reciting Thoreau the same way other kids did the Pledge of Allegiance or John 3:16—

"It's not what you look at that matters. It's what you see."

"You must live in the present, launch yourself on every wave, find your eternity in each moment."

"How vain it is to sit down and write when you have not stood up to live."

—and now picture me nearly two decades later: in my pajamas, in New Orleans, reciting Thoreau's words over and over as Abe gave me the address.

What would Henry say?

He'd say, *Get your ass to the Funky Butt.*

(Except he probably wouldn't say *ass*.)

I stepped out of the hotel and was shocked to see the streets so alive—I thought I'd be alone in the dark like Chicago at that time, but this was the French Quarter and there were people everywhere, laughing and drinking, walking with arms locked and greeting complete strangers like they'd known each other all their lives. "Here honey, you need some of this!" said a bead-draped redhead, handing me a Styrofoam cup filled with some kind of fruity daiquiri. I'd soon learn that if I walked into one of the numerous, open-all-night liquor booths on every cobblestone corner, I could refill that Styrofoam cup for a dollar. I stood there in front of my hotel, drinking that daquiri like it was juice and watching the crowd pulse around me. That's when I heard the music.

Granted, music was coming from everywhere—the bars and stores and second-story balcony windows—but this was different. This was coming from the next street, right around the corner, and I followed the sound. The strange thing was, it *moved.* I rounded the corner and could hear that I'd just missed it so I rounded the next corner, and the next, all the corners of cobblestone streets set like a labyrinth and all the while the music was getting louder until finally—

There.

A marching band.

A full marching band at three o'clock in the morning. They were all suited up, duck-bill hats and feathered plumes, spats on the boots, and a hundred buttons. There were trumpets and drums and trombones and clarinets with Dixieland sound, fifty people strong all step-marching and moving their instruments in rhythm. There was a crowd of people following behind them, everybody dancing and trying to copy the choreographed marching movements. I could feel the daquiri icy in my head, and it was so late, maybe I was still sleeping, maybe I was dreaming and you can do anything in a dream, right?—so I did it. I joined. "I don't remember the last time I danced!" I yelled to the guy next to me. He was wearing a giant foam carrot on his head. "That's the saddest thing I ever heard!" he yelled, and then we laughed, and I couldn't remember the last time I'd laughed, either. I suddenly felt this rush—the rush of the repressed, we'll call it—and I ran around the band, passed them on the sidewalk and shimmied into the street in front of them. I marched high, my knees coming up level to my stomach, and tossed an imaginary baton in the air.

That's when I saw the street the concierge had told me to take, so I walked backward and waved goodbye to the drum major. He smiled, I skipped off down my street, and—

They followed me. The entire band and the growing crowd behind them followed me around another corner, and another. And another. And of *course* I wasn't really leading them, of *course* I was just walking the same route they were taking, *of course!* but sometimes, we have to believe the fantastic.

I got to the Funky Butt—a wild, second-floor jazz club over a jam-packed cigar bar—waved goodbye to my band, and ran up the stairs to find Abe. He was dancing in a sweaty, sardine-packed crowd, and I rushed over to tell him my news.

"I led a marching band!" I yelled.

"I lit my pants on fire!" he yelled back, and put a shot in my hands. And then another, and another, and dancing all night long, me and Abe and a million people I'd never met but somehow knew. My boss was there, too, smoking cigars and spinning pretty girls around in circles. He dipped me low to the ground and, when I was down there, inches from the floor, he asked, "Having fun?" Fun, *fun*—who knew! I didn't, not me, not this girl, who was this girl I had suddenly become? One thing's for sure—she was *way* more interesting than the one at the erotic poetry seminar.

For the record: I love erotic poetry. I love poetry, period. And novels, period. And short stories and essays, all of it, erotic essays, even! I don't care what you call it or where you shelve it or what it gets printed on, I just want the words, the ideas, and the stories handed to me like birthday presents. I want to find my own feelings in someone else's experiences. I want to live lives I couldn't possibly have lived, exist in a reality that can't possibly be real—that's what a story can do.

"What about your actual life?" asked my therapist.

"Do you want to have dinner this weekend?" asked Dan.

"Having fun?" asked my department chair.

"You want some crepes?" asked Abe. *Ask-yell-slurred*—and I felt that happens when wild, drunken abandonment becomes a slobbery, drunken mess. My head was throbbing, the music was too loud, who were all these people sweating all over me?

"I have to go!" I yelled at Abe.

"No, stay! There's an all-night crepe place! We'll have mimosas!" he yelled back, but I was already running down the stairs, out the door, into the street and—

There they were.

The trombones. The clarinets. The drums—all of them lined up in perfect rows, all of them frozen still in attention, all of them watching the drum major's hands. They were suspended in the air, tense and ready, but his head was turned to me. "Whenever you're ready," he said—I could only see his mouth. The rest of his face was hidden under a giant, duck-billed helmet with a long feather plume.

"Ready for what?" I whispered.

"This," he said, dropping his hands, and it all began again, fast as a needle scratch on a record: the explosion of sound, a crowd appearing from nowhere, everyone dancing in crazy, synchronized choreography, costumes made of feathers and sequins, and—high above the quarter— the sun started to climb the sky. "You look like you need this," said a bead-draped brunette, handing me another Styrofoam cup, and Abe appeared at my elbow. "Fuck," he said. "You really do have a band!"

Then he grabbed my hand and we jumped into the street, tossing our batons as we went.

I don't remember the rest of that trip. I don't remember the flight to Chicago, the cab ride home to Humboldt Park. What I do remember was my blaring alarm clock at 6:00 a.m., the jackhammers pounding in my temples, and, for some reason, this stupid discussion I'd had in grad school that escalated into a stupid fight. I said that if the writing was good enough, you could live the experience through the words and never need to have it for yourself. "Why do I need to drink? I've read Hemingway! I've read *Beowulf*! I know what drinking feels like! Here, look at this passage from Kingsley Amis describing a hangover. It's perfect! It's poetry! I don't ever need to have one!"

I went on.

And on and on.

I was insufferable in grad school. I knew everything in grad school, except the fact that I didn't know shit. My jackhammers were not Kingsley Amis. My experiences were not *Finnegans Wake*. My life didn't exist inside a conference room. It was here, in Chicago, with the jackhammers and the alarm clock, so I showered quickly and ran down the front stairs with my hair still wet. In the front hallway, I searched for my car keys, hoping I didn't forget anything, coffee, I forgot coffee, I needed coffee, and I threw open the door—

And there they were.

On my tiny square of lawn was the marching band from New Orleans. Same duck-billed hats, same spats, same dancing crowd behind them. Their music blended in with the West Side noise—the traffic and yelling and little kids screaming and—

I shut the door.

It can't be, I thought, and opened the door.

—the music swelled again, loud and joyful, and—

I shut the door. Just how many brain cells had I killed with those fruity Louisiana daiquiris? I peeked through the peephole. The band waited patiently, instruments at the ready. I cracked the door just a little bit and—

The drum major dropped his hands and the sound exploded.

I slammed the door this time. Hard. Then I ran back upstairs, through my apartment, out the back door, and down the back stairs. I can shake them, I thought. Just gotta be fast enough, gotta—

Bastards, there they were! That fucking band, all lined up in formation, instruments at the ready. The drum major's hands were in the air, and he tilted his feather in my direction. "Whenever you're ready," he said. I looked back toward my apartment with its bed and books and locks, and then out to the band. The sun was climbing behind them, over the alley, the three-flats, my city. I thought of that morning in New Orleans and how much fun I'd had. I thought of my students and what I wanted to teach them about writing, and all of a sudden, I felt that click: when avoiding your life becomes more difficult than actually living it.

"Fine," I told the drum major. "But no 'Saints Go Marching In.'" His feather nodded and, in one fluid motion, he lifted up on his toes and dropped his whole body.

Humboldt Park didn't know what hit it.

Since then, they follow me everywhere. They're there—in the produce section at the Jewel. Near the free-weights at the Y. Pumping gas at the Citgo. When I'm teaching, they stand in a line at the back of my classroom, and whenever I make a joke about the Oxford comma the drummer does a *BA-BA-BAM!* When I get on the El to go home, they're there, playing Dixieland for the commuters. When Dan comes over for dinner, they play—something slow. Sultry. They're rooting for me. They've become a part of how I do things. Like, I'll be running late but it doesn't matter, I have to stop and listen. Even now, as I write this, I can see them out of the corner of my eye: all of them dancing in my living room, their helmets a carpet of waving feathers. They want me to loosen up a little. Shake my shoulders, give a little shimmy. Later tonight, we'll go out—you're welcome to come—and I'll lead everyone down the street, Humboldt to North Avenue and Ashland from there. We'll pick up a crowd as we go, and all of us will dance in the street.

One One-Thousand,
Two One-Thousand, Three

Eliza was fourteen when she moved out of Climax. Mom and Dad split up, Dad got the house, Mom the kid, and within a month Eliza was packing up her bedroom in secondhand tomato boxes from Kroger's. Her story could fit into one of those boxes.

She didn't mind moving too much, crossing her fingers that her home-to-be in Iowa would be different than Climax—thirty miles west of Cereal City and empty as one of the ghost towns in the late-night rodeo flicks she watched when nightmares kept her wide awake and shivering during Michigan Februarys. She wouldn't miss those Februarys. She wouldn't miss the 4H fairs either, or the Mom and Dad fights in the kitchen when they thought she was sleeping, or the nose-stuck-to-the-wind girls at Climax Junior High, who all thought they were so damn better just 'cause their daddies had businesses on Main Street, their boyfriends got the keys to pickup trucks on Friday nights, and their new bras had little fabric roses in the center and "You don't need one of these yet, huh Eliza?" they'd say, and giggle, and Eliza would pull her little-girl undershirt over her head and wonder why she was always two steps behind.

There was one thing Eliza would miss. About two miles out of Climax, close enough for her to get to on her bike, was a quarry. Hidden safe inside a coven-circle of trees was a pool of green water near as big as a baseball field, all sunk down into the belly of mineral walls with ledges about fifteen feet up from the water. There was a flat dip in the ledge over on the southwest side, low enough for Eliza to drop her Levi's and

Albion College sweatshirts, tennis shoes, and jockeys into neat folded piles and dive into the water; a long, clean smooth dive that would have secured her a spot on the CHS swim team (they almost won the state championship back in '87!). She would kick hard under the seaweedy water—fancying herself a mermaid in its glow—push herself as far as her breath would carry, and then fly sputtering to the surface, laughing aloud and diving back underneath like a waterbird. This was Eliza's place, always empty in the daytime with the sun gleaming off the pool and lighting it up like a vanity-table mirror. She would flip onto her back, spread-eagle style like she was making snow angels, and float across the water feeling like Aphrodite or Ophelia or any of those silly adolescent girls swimming naked in the sunshine thinking achy poetic things. She always thought that when she met her Mr. Someone, she'd take him there with her, let her special spot become theirs, a together kinda place instead of a lonely kinda place.

Now, she'd never admit it to you, but Eliza always kinda fantasized that Mr. Someone might find her there, just happen upon her one day dead-man's floating across the pool with her yellow hair splayed around her head like a fan and her body glowing phosphorescent white, and fall head-over-heels like men always did in Jane Austen novels.

She'd imagine him standing up on the ledge behind a tree, watching her in secret, his face hot-red and his pulse thump-kicking in his chest. Every day he'd hide behind those trees, hoping that she'd be there, hoping to catch a glimpse of her. For that reason alone, Eliza always washed her hair before going to her secret place. She kept her fingernails neat and trimmed, too, and wore pink lip gloss. She wanted to be pretty when he finally came for her.

The day before she and her mom loaded all the boxes into the rented U-Haul, Eliza biked out to the quarry for one last swim. It was a hot day at the tag end of August and she was sweating something heavy from the ride by the time she got there, climbing down the ledge to the base of the pool. She wanted to jump right in but instead made herself take it slow, burning every moment into her brain so she'd be able to summon it up in her memory in Iowa: the silence, the peace, the green of the water, the powerful feel of the sun on her naked chest as she peeled off her tank-top and unbuttoned her shorts, letting them drop to her ankles and pushing her panties after. She shut her eyes and lifted her arms behind her head, first unknotting the ponytail that caught up her long yellow hair, and then lifting her arms up to the sky. If anyone had been watching her, they would have seen an adolescent girl with knobby knees and a straight-as-an-arrow body. But standing there with her eyes closed and hot-red fire dots appearing on the backs of her lids, her hands raised heavenward, her hair brushing rumpled against the base of her spine, Eliza felt beautiful and grown-up and not-of-this-world. It was a moment she needed to be alone for, a moment without inhibition or fear or all her silly schoolgirl hang-ups.

But Eliza wasn't alone.

She dove into the water, which exploded cold and delicious across her body. She kicked down deep, holding her breath in her cheeks like chipmunks', swimming in S curves around the base of the pool where the water was icy and dark forest-green. When her temples started pulsing in the sides of her forehead and her mouth felt like she'd been blowing up party balloons, Eliza pushed herself toward the surface and the warm stale air, bursting through the glassy top of the water and sucking it in with fat chesty gasps. Once her breathing calmed, she treaded in place and rubbed the water out of her eyes before opening them.

That was when she saw him.

It was hard to see exactly, the sun was so bright, but she knew it was a guy from the tennis shoes and cut-off shorts, knew it from the way his biceps shoved out of his T-shirt like baseballs, knew it from the way he stared at her, mesmerized.

You'd think her first thought would have been fear, like *Oh my God, naked alone with a man in the middle of nowhere!* Or maybe humiliation, like *Oh my God, he saw me naked!* Or maybe logic, like *Oh my God, I've got to swim over to the shallow end and get into my clothes right quick!* Eliza didn't think of any of those things. What she thought was this: *It's him.* Him as in the faceless guy she thought about before she fell asleep at night. Him as in the guy you see standing next to you when you're forty and fat with little yellow-haired kids. Him as in the Mr. Someone that you always wait for, and compare everyone else to, and pine for, and hope for, and cry about. And for exactly two seconds Eliza locked her blue eyes on this silhouette of man-of-my-dreams, and dropped hopelessly into little-girl love.

And then the third second ticked by and another guy showed up at Mr. Someone's elbow, this next one sunburned and shirtless, sporting his high-school quarterback chest and swiggin' from a can of Old Style that somebody's older brother must have bought for him. "Yee-HAW!" he cried when he made it to the tip of the ledge and noticed Eliza naked in the water. "Whatja got here, cuz!" His voice echoed around the quarry and he slapped his knee in delight, the same kind of joy he'd get finding his dad's *Penthouse* magazines lying around the living room. "Hey y'all!" he called over his shoulder. "Come see what Wes found!"

Eliza looked back at the first boy, half hoping for him to take a gilded sword out of his pocket and drive it through this enemy's chest . . . I mean, after all, she'd shared the most beautiful two seconds of her life with him, had been coming here for years on the slim chance he'd bust up out of her imagination as a real flesh-and-blood perfect person. And now, here he was, with his hands stuck way down deep in his pockets, looking back and forth between Eliza and his friend like he didn't know what to do, and, *Duh, instead of having to make a decision I guess I'll just do nothin'.*

That's when Eliza felt all those things that should have punctured her gut from the get-go: humiliation and helplessness and dull raw fear. Boys were coming out from the circle of trees, two more of them, four more, five more, six, till there was almost a baseball team (starters *and* relief) lined up single-file on the edge of the ledge and looking down at Eliza like she was a seal at Shedd Aquarium, hootin' and hollerin' and slapping their thighs, chug-a-lugging on their beer cans and giggling like they'd just tapped into the free-porn channel on cable access.

Eliza back-paddled slowly, barely disturbing the water around her, until she was crouched down in the shallow end of the pool with her knees locked into her chest and her long hair plastered wet to her back. Sitting there was agony, pure and shameful with red-hot embarrassment flooding her cheeks, but even worse would be to leave. In order to leave, see, she'd have to stand, and run over to her clothes, and the thought of putting her little-girl nakedness on display made her ache down to the tips of her toes. No, getting up with them watching her like a Coney Island freak was out of the question, but she couldn't stay, either; remaining in that water like a chicken in a boiling pot sent panic creeping up the back of her spine.

46

"C'mon baby!" they called, slugging one another in the upper arms and reaching for more beer. "C'mon, stand up! We just want to see you is all!" Everything inside Eliza tensed. She tightened her arms around her chest and watched her thighs glow white under the water, trying to focus her eyes down, not wanting to look up, not wanting to let her fear escape her, not wanting them to see it along with everything else she held secret and alone.

"We just wanna see you!" yelled the shirtless boy.

"Yeah!" yelled another, and yet another saluted her with his empty beer can and promised, "We ain't gonna do anything to you or anything! We just wanna *look*!"

Eliza sat there, frozen still, and waited for the anger to come, for some kind of survival instinct to kick in and propel her forward. She let her eyes lift up to the first boy, the one they'd called Wes. He was standing back from his friends, twisting his foot into the dusty ground and looking nervous. Then he looked up, and for another two seconds his eyes locked onto Eliza's. One one-thousand, two one-thousand—

"*Get up!*" yelled the shirtless boy, and there was something different in his tone now, something that was not playing around anymore, and he stood as far down the ledge as he could without falling over. The rest of them picked up the beat. "Get up! Get up! *Get up!*"—they yelled it like they were at a basketball game cheering for defense—and "C'mon, baby, we just wanna look is all!" like they were nice boys spending a nice afternoon at the art museum or something, and when that didn't work they said, "We're not waiting around this long for nothing, you know," like she was failing to fulfill her end of the bargain, and when that didn't work they pleaded with her, saying "C'mon, sugar, you're *killing* us here!" like this was all her fault and then finally, after they'd dropped to the ground and sat with their legs hanging over the ledge like little boys on too-high stools: "You'll get cold sometime, honey!" and there they all sat, everybody waiting.

Eliza stared at her hands, small and smooth and spotted with sunburn-freckles, slowly shriveling with water-wrinkles like raisins, the skin around her fingernails pasty white and brittle like the insides of a grape. She squatted in the water for hours and the sun started to drop; the sky turned pale purple, and she tightened her skinny arms around her chest and tried to control her shivering. A small fist of fear in her middle expanded throughout her body. One one-thousand, two one-thousand, three one-thousand—and she stared up at Wes and pretended it was just the two of them.

"Goddammit!" yelled the shirtless boy suddenly, and Eliza gritted her teeth and winced as he smashed an empty forty bottle against the side of the ledge and stood up. "I'm sick of waiting. We been waitin for fuckin' ever, it's fuckin'—" His words slurred together and he looked around at his friends, trying to fuse his mind into some sort of decision. "Fuck it," he said, first to them, and then a second time yelled down the ledge at her; "*Fuck* it. *Fuck. It.*" He waited for a beat or two, as if giving Eliza one last chance to stand up. She didn't, and he broke. "I'm gonna go get her," he slobbered. "Jimmy," he said, spinning aimlessly around, looking for his friend, "Jimmy, we're gonna go get her. We're gonna go get her, this is fuckin' shit waiting for all this fuckin'—" and again he cut himself off, pointing his left arm in a clockwise circumference of the quarry. "I'm gonna go around like this," he said, and then flung his right arm around in the other direction, "and you're gonna go around like that and we're gonna get her in the middle. *Didja hear that?*" he yelled down at Eliza, who looked up at Wes—one one-thousand, two one-thousand, three one-thousand—"*Ya got all that, honey?*" The gaggle of guys all laughed stupid drunken laughs. "*Honey!*" he yelled, encouraged by the laughter, "*I'm comin' down there, honey! Me 'n you, honey!*" And he laughed at himself and started stumbling left, signaling Jimmy to go right.

Eliza watched the two of them circle around her like vultures on dead things. Even if she wanted to run now, she couldn't. They'd be sure to reach her before she could climb up over the ledge, and, even so, she was freezing and shivering and there wasn't anymore fight in her.

She heard it then, heard, "C'mon, Lee, leave her alone," and as she lifted her eyes she saw Wes following Lee around the perimeter of the pool. "C'mon, Lee," he kept repeating, "C'mon Lee, don't." His voice was quiet, barely audible over Eliza's chattering teeth. He stood a good head shorter than Lee and had to take a double step to compensate for every one of his drunken strides, but still he kept up.

"Don't *what?*" yelled Lee. His voice was terrible.

"Don't go down there, man," said Wes, throwing in the 'man' as an afterthought, like it might calm Lee down, keeping his eyes focused on the distance between Lee and Eliza.

48

"Don't go down there, *man*," Lee mimicked in a sing-song voice, as he reached Eliza's ledge and prepared for the climb down.

Wes grabbed ahold of Lee's upper arm and held on tight. "I'm serious," he said. Eliza was almost directly below them, ten short feet down. Now that he was closer he could see that she was shivering, that her lips were blue.

Lee looked at Wes's hand on his arm as if he couldn't understand what it was doing there. His eyes were bloodshot and his voice was low, growling. "You need to let me go," he said, some horrible intimidation, but Wes held his ground and shook his head. "You need to leave her alone," he said, taking a step backward from Lee but not loosening his grip.

Lee looked back at the hand that was still on his arm. "You need to not piss me off," he said, inflating himself to full height and looking down at Wes, his body tense, cocked.

"Leave her alone," Wes said again.

Lee's eyes burned blue. "Look," he said, his voice suddenly Mr. Nice Guy, "I know you're new here and all, Wes, and I know you've been through some shit, what with your mom and all. *That's* why I'm being so nice about this." His words slurred together and his eyes were unfocused. "*That's* why I'm giving you one last chance to let me go before I get upset. You know, we're cousins and all," and with his free arm he reached out and patted Wes on the shoulder, a friendly, brotherly sort of pat. Pat pat pat.

Wes's jaw was tense. "Not until you leave her alone," he said.

The patting turned hard, violent thrusts into Wes's upper arm. "I said, *let go of me*," Lee roared, and Wes held on tight. "No," he said, and steeled himself for what he knew was coming next. The first punch landed on his temple and the second in his eye. *Dthoom Dthoom*, dull pain and Wes hit the ground, instinctively wrapping his hands around his head and curling in his knees to protect his stomach, waiting for the kicks that he knew would follow the punches, hard in the gut, and Wes gritted his teeth and gasped.

Lee's breath came faster and he spat out words with every kick. "Told—you—" slamming his foot into Wes's stomach, once, twice— "not to fuck—" slamming into his groin—"with—" his chest—"*me*—" slamslamslam and Wes bit down hard on his lip, tasting blood—"You think you can show up in *my* life—" and Lee was down on the ground, flipping Wes over on his back and straddling him, leaning so close that Wes could smell the beer on his breath, holding the collar of Wes's T-shirt in one tight fist and punching him with the other: the eye, nose, mouth, jaw, *Dthoom Dthoom Dthoom* darkness.

All Wes saw when he opened his eyes were stars—not stars like little cartoon ones that float around your head when you've had the shit knocked out of you, but honest-to-goodness aurora borealis stars, constellations spread out on the sky above the quarry like the astronomy map in Earth Science class. He lay there for a moment, looking up, taking it all in, until the inevitable *why am I lying on my back on a rock?* question showed up somewhere in his battered brain. He stood up real fast—balking at the pain, bending over at the waist and taking a few deep breaths—when he remembered, his head hurting more from imagining what they'd done to her than it did from what they really did to him. He looked around, panicked—they were gone, no drunken yells. All he could hear was the crickets starting their evening hum. Desperately afraid they'd taken her with them, he ran to the ledge and peered over.

She was there, still in the same squatting position in the shallow water—now stained midnight blue without the sun—her back to him, still as stone.

"It's okay," he said, relief washing over him, "it's okay, they've gone. You can get out." He stood there staring at her back, wondering why she wasn't moving. Was she hurt? Did she have—what was it called? hypothermia?—from sitting in there for so long? It was nighttime now, the sky black and starry and a thin strip of moonlight swiping the pool and illuminating her like a spotlight. Then it hit him suddenly—she wasn't going to get up with him there, either. He was one of them to her, not a lick different than Lee and the rest. He'd been watching her, too, he was the reason why any of this had happened.

"I'll leave," he called down. "I'm sorry, I never thought that . . . I won't—" and he couldn't figure out how to say it without sounding like all the rest of them— "watch," he finished weakly. "I won't look at you if you don't want me to," and he was all set to turn when she stood up.

It was hard to stand. She'd been sitting for so long that her joints had stiffened up. She felt tingles in her legs and warm air on her thighs and his eyes on her back. This was what she had waited all day for: not for the rest of them to leave, no, that was too simple. She'd wanted to get back to that moment with him, to see what would happen if they got to the third second. She turned around slowly, letting him take in all of her with his eyes: the backs of her knees and her butt and her spiky shoulder blades, her narrow hips and square waist; she was all straight lines and right angles, but as she turned in the moonlight for that fifteen-year-old boy on the top of the ledge, she felt full and rich and curvy, beautiful and sexy and desirable and all those things that women wait their whole lives for and sometimes never experience.

Face-to-face, eye-to-eye, one one-thousand, two one-thousand, three. Eliza stood calf-deep in the water and stared up at him. His eye was black and his lip bloody, his jaw dropped down into his chest as he stared at her, wide-eyed, scared and excited. "I was just watching you," he stammered, looking away and then looking back, as if some invisible force was pulling his head from side to side, as if he knew he shouldn't be looking at her but just couldn't tear his eyes away, that terrible-wonderful feeling you have when you make love with the lights on for the very first time. "I didn't want any of this to happen," he said, "I mean, I just wanted to . . . see you."

Eliza rested her fingertips against her thighs and let him see, conscious the whole time of keeping her arms at her sides and her chin high. She wanted him to see every part of her, every inch, every line. For the first time in her life she didn't have any shame, and she wanted it to last as long as humanly possible. Moving slowly, she stepped up onto the low ledge and walked silvery and naked across the rocks, getting closer and closer. She tilted her head farther back as she neared the rock wall, trying to keep him in her line of vision, until she reached the base and he was out of sight. *He's up there*, she thought, sticking fingers and bare feet into the wall and starting to climb. Left hand, right hand, left foot, right, and pebbles pinched her hands and jagged stone cut at her feet, but to a fourteen-year-old girl so close to Mr. Someone—ten feet, nine feet, eight feet, seven—none of that mattered. She didn't know what would happen once she reached the top, just knew she had been waiting for that moment for her whole life—three feet, two feet, one—her left hand reaching over the top of the ledge, seeking something to grasp, her right hand following, the excitement almost unbearable, pounding at her chest and, using the all the strength left in her small, underdeveloped body, she hefted herself on her upper arms and pulled herself to her knees on top of the ledge and—this may have been the bravest thing she ever did— looked up.

Missed Connection

Last Friday, Trader Joe's checkout aisle. You: six feet, blue eyes, blue Hawaiian shirt, your name tag said Ted. Me: five-seven, blonde, gray sweater, I handed you my groceries so you could scan their bar codes: Coffee. *Bleep*. Oranges. *Bleep*. You didn't look up at me, just kept working. Hummus. *Bleep*. Pita. *Bleep*. "How are you tonight?" you asked. Gouda. *Bleep*. "Paper or plastic?"

"Paper," I said, and you scanned the grapes. *Bleep*. The pretzels. *Bleep*. The eggs—and this is where time slowed down. You picked up the eggs and looked at me—quick at first, like any retail guy looking at his customer—*No big deal, right?*—but then something changed, and I know this might sound stupid but it was like in that movie *Big Fish*: Ewan McGregor's at the circus and there are all these clowns and midgets and dancing poodles, and then he sees this girl, and everything freezes. He walks toward her and she's all beautiful, blonde hair and big eyes and blue frilly dress, and he just stands there, staring at her and it's like *Yes. This is it. This is the moment that will change my life forever. I'm staring at this girl and I don't want to know what will happen next because it can't possibly be as great as this*—which is when you dropped the eggs, all of them spilling out over your scanner and cracking, oozing gooey yolk all over your hands. Still, you didn't look away. You stared at me and I stared back and it's been a long time since a man has reacted to me that way. The last time was at a baseball game in Humboldt Park. Gary was playing right field and I was walking my dog. I passed him at the exact moment a line drive shot along first, but Gary was watching me so he missed the ball. His teammates started yelling at him and he ran back to collect it outside

53

the chalked baselines, and as he jogged back he stopped to ask for my number. I lent him a Sharpie and he wrote it on his glove. That was three years ago, and we just broke up. He moved everything out last month, but he left that goddamn glove. To torture me? I don't know. Every night I stare at it. Every moment I think about it, right up until you dropped the eggs, Ted, and then I wasn't thinking about anything but you.

That's when Steven came up behind me, and you broke the stare. You averted your eyes and started apologizing like crazy, mopping up the egg yolk with paper towels. I understand why you did that. You thought he was my boyfriend, and of course you would think that! Look at our groceries: Bottles of wine. Two steaks, two sweet potatoes, breakfast food for the morning after. And Steven is not one of those gay guys you can tell is gay just by looking at him. I mean, he's not very flashy. He had on jeans and a Cubs T-shirt—a *Cubs* T-shirt! Like he's a *Cubs* fan! "What do you want me to wear to Trader Joe's?" he asked later. "Pink pinstripes?"

"No," I said. "But you could've been—"

"What?" he said. "A little *gayer*?" Like I wanted him to sing *Gypsy* in the middle of Trader Joe's or something, which is totally not the case, Ted. I just wanted you to know the truth and it's not like I could jump up on the checkout counter and yell, "It's not like that! He's my *friend*, you don't have to stop looking at me like you want to high-jump your cash register and take me behind the stacked Rotini boxes!"

"Long night?" Steven said to you as he bagged up our groceries, and you said, "Not so bad, I get off in an hour"—and then you looked at me like what you really meant was *Do you want to ditch this bozo and meet me at the Leopard Lounge?* and I tried to look back like *Yes, Ted, I will meet you at the Leopard Lounge*, and that's when Steven turned to me and said, "You've got my wallet, sweetheart."

Sweetheart.

You broke our stare and went back to the groceries. "Looks like you two have a nice weekend planned," you said, and I heard the sarcasm in your voice—don't think I wasn't tuned into it, I was tuned into everything about you by that point: the muscles in your forearms and your square jaw and your mouth and Steven said, "Yep. We're getting out of town," and you said, "Isn't that *nice*! Where to?"

"Michigan," I said, and you said, "Where in Michigan?"

"Holland," I said, and you said, "I'm from South Haven!" and I know that here in Chicago we run into people from Michigan every day, holding up our palms to make the mitten, but in that moment, Ted, it felt like something special, something rare, and we just stood there staring at each other for, like, ever, maybe, until the woman in line behind me started clearing her throat and I didn't know what to say so I said, "Uhm, have a good night," and what you said was, "Have a good weekend," but what you meant was, *We are from the same land, you and I. Our bodies hum with the electric harmony of Michigan. Slice open our veins and there, pumping hot toward our hearts, is Sparky Anderson, cherry wine, and the Christmas glory of Frankenmuth*, and I picked up the paper bags Steven wasn't already holding and we left.

"Are you crazy?" he said, when we got to the car. "Why didn't you give that guy your number?"

"He wasn't interested in me," I said, even though I knew you were, Ted. I could feel it in my toes.

"You didn't even try," Steven said, which is something he's been saying a lot lately what with Gary and everything. It was making me kind of mad, to tell you the truth, and I said, "I *did* try," which is sort of snippy, I know. Usually I'm not like that, Ted.

Steven studied my face. "Are we talking about Gary again? I thought we were done with him."

"I am! But—"

"Okay, then!" he said. "So go back in there and talk to the grocery guy! He's really cute!" which you really are, Ted, especially if Steven thinks so because he has impeccable taste in men, most gay men do. It's girls like me who run after the bad ones. Like Gary. Who's in a band. A kind of famous one. I mean, maybe you've heard of them, Ted. Maybe I'll say the name and you'll be like, *No way! I fuckin' love them!* and then I'll have to die a little bit because whenever I think of his music now, I think of the show he played a few months ago in Madison. I thought I'd drive up and surprise him, you know? Like, *look how much I love you, I drove three hours in the rain*—so much rain that I was drenched just from running between the car and the club. I walked in, paid my five bucks—I wouldn't have been on the list because Gary didn't know I was coming, remember?—and pushed through the packed, darkened, drunken crowd with their cigarettes and PBRs and ear-splitting music and then I saw him, at the other side of the room, with this girl. They were kissing, and there's this thing that happens in your stomach when you see something like that—it freezes on the inside, like if someone punched you just then you'd hear breaking glass. I walked over to them and stood there, watching. They didn't even notice me. So finally I said, "Hey," and they both looked at me, but he didn't do anything. His girl looked back and forth between him and me, trying to figure out what was going on, so I introduced myself. There was no recognition in her face, no *This is Gary's girlfriend*. She had no idea, but she did have manners, 'cause she said "Hey," and I looked back at my boyfriend. I thought of his stuff in our apartment. I thought of my Sunday afternoon conversations with his mother. I thought of the photographs of the two of us together on the fridge, but I saw none of that in his face.

"Okay," I said aloud. "Okay, Gary, I get it," and then I turned my back.

So when Steven said, "Go back in there and talk to that grocery guy!" you can certainly understand, Ted, why I didn't.

"I'm not ready," I said, and then I started the car; away from the parking lot, away from you, and Steven leaned back in the passenger seat and sighed, which in Stevenspeak translates into *Fine whatever just ruin your whole goddamn life. Again.*

Steven and I spend one weekend a month at my dad's place in Holland. It's on the beach, so in the summer we can swim and in the winter sit by the fire and relax, listening to the lake's winds pound the walls. Gary never minded that I spent so much time with another man—there is, after all, no chance of sex with Steven. We share a bed and nothing happens. We go away together on the weekends and my fidelity is not questioned.

Whaddya mean you're going away with some guy?
He's gay?
Okay then. It's cool.

It's funny, Ted, how you boys are so threatened by who might possess my body but care nothing about who's got my heart. Steven knows everything about me—every hope and fear and dream. He knows the lies I tell people and why I tell them. He knows the things I've never told. Doesn't that seem silly, Ted? That the man I am not sleeping with knows the purpose for my existence and the man I am sleeping with knows—I was going to say my favorite movie but I don't know if Gary knew that.

It's *Big Fish*. In case you're interested.

"You have to be ready sometime," Steven said as we hit I-94 East out of the city, and I didn't mean to do it, Ted, I don't know where it came from, but I started to cry. I cried so hard that I had to pull over on the shoulder and turn on the parking lights, and Steven and I switched passenger and driver seats. Then we were moving again, toward the Skyway, Steven behind the wheel and me a floodgate with the windshield wipers on the wrong side of the windshield.

He let me cry for a while. Then he said, "What's happening to you, sweetheart?"

"I don't know," I cried. "It's just that—" and then I brought up all these things that Steven has long since known: childhood and past relationships and too much time thinking too hard; so much information that I don't know you well enough to get into here, Ted, and maybe that's why I'm writing this. I want to know if I can get into it with you. That look we shared? Over the cracked eggs? Was that about something more? If so, you can leave me a message at this email. We can get some coffee, maybe. Or breakfast. I could scramble the eggs. Make something good out of the destruction.

The Flood

Later, we'll study this day in history class. Books will have been written, documentaries made, references dropped in political speeches and scientific research. It'll be like April 4 or September 11, our first steps on the moon, the Challenger Explosion, Hurricane Katrina; everyone remembers exactly what they were doing the moment it happened.

I was in my apartment, a second-floor walk-up on Logan Boulevard. It was August, one of those unbearably hot Chicago Augusts, and my son, Nick, was sunburned from his ears to the waistband of his shorts. I remember putting aloe on his back and being surprised by how big he was, how grown. Soon he'd be leaving for college and I wasn't quite sure what to *do* with myself. I had him when I was nineteen, brought him up alone, there was never time to *do* anything besides survive, and now?

What would I do now?

"Hey, Mom," Nick said. "What's that?" I looked from his back to the window and that's when I saw it: delicate white cotton balls, like someone cut open a pillow and shook out its stuffing.

"Is it from the air conditioner?" Nick asked. At first I was surprised he didn't recognize it, but if you do the math, he was only five years old the last time it snowed, and I suddenly realized how much time had passed.

"It's snow," I told him.

"Yeah, right," he said. "It hasn't snowed in like ten years."

"Twelve," I said. He turned to look at me, seeing the truth in my face. "No *way!*" he yelled, and was out the door, forgetting the sunburn in his rush to see: snow.

I moved closer to the window and watched it fall, feeling suddenly nostalgic. I thought of hot chocolate, making snowmen with my dad, the light displays at Lincoln Park Zoo, and, most of all, Joe—all those things I'd loved about winter before the snow stopped falling and things got so goddamn hard.

The first time Joe left I was nineteen and had just told him I was pregnant. He didn't say anything, just stood up and went to the bathroom. "What should we do?" I asked, watching as he climbed fully dressed into the shower, the water weighing down his clothes till I knew he was too heavy for me to hold up alone. I was already overloaded with the plastic stick turned pink and a heartbeat in my stomach. "Couldn't be the heartbeat," the doctor told me later. "It's too soon to feel the heartbeat. It's not scientifically possible"—but I've never once believed in the infallibility of science.

Eight months later, right before Christmas, I called Joe's voicemail from the hospital. "It's a boy," I said. Then I went to sleep.

The next day, the nurse said I had a visitor. "He's been here all morning," she said. "Still here," she said after lunch, and the same before dinner. I'd been counting snowflakes out the window and right before visiting hours closed I grabbed her wrist. "Tell him . . . I said okay."

The first day home, Joe bundled Nicky in a blanket and took him outside to see the snow.

The second day, we went back to the hospital 'cause Nick was sneezing.

The third day, Joe was gone. He'd left a note that said, *He'll be better off.*

The next note came a year later, just after Nick's first birthday. We did Christmas at my mom's, and hanging on her tree was an envelope with a check, a phone number, and a question: *Can I see him?* I looked at the words for a long time. Then I went to the phone.

Nick and I had just moved into the two-flat on Logan; not much to look at, but I could afford it with waitress shifts and there was a little scrap of front yard with clean, unspoiled snow. Joe held Nicky up to touch icicles while I watched from the porch. Maybe it would work out, I thought. We'd be a family: me, Joe, and our little boy. Maybe later there'd be a girl, too. Maybe some dogs. Move somewhere warm like Florida or San Diego. We'd have a swimming pool in the backyard and every year we'd take a picture, all of us sitting on the diving board, smiling—that was my fantasy. So when Joe asked if he could put Nicky to bed, I said okay. And when he asked if he could stay awhile, I said fine. We sat on opposite sides of the living room, saying nothing, and after a thousand hours I moved next to him and put my head on his shoulder.

He lasted a few weeks that time, and then was gone. The snow stopped and started again, and in between Nicky talked. His first word was *Ma*. After that, in quick succession: *suture*, *swab*, and *capillary*. I'd started nursing school and would study aloud with Nicky before bed; then I'd drop him at my mom's and go to work. The night he turned two I was walking from the car to the house, Nicky fast asleep and slung over my shoulder, and when I looked up—there was Joe.

"Can I see him?" he asked.

No. Get out. I miss you. I'm tired. Those were all answers I could've given in that moment and any of them would've been true. I stayed silent, turning till Joe could see Nick's little face over my shoulder, and imagined that family on the diving board. I could have that family. Right?

He left a few days later; no foreshadowing the departure, no forewarning the return. On Nick's third birthday, he ran to his father sitting on the porch. On his fourth, he hid behind my legs. On his fifth, he sat at the kitchen table stacking Cheerios and said, "You know what, Mom? I get the shaft."

I'd been decorating cupcakes for him to take to school; now I gripped the counter to brace myself.

"Kids who got birthdays in summer get more presents," he went on, and I exhaled, relieved. I wasn't ready for the Joe conversation. I'd never be ready for the Joe conversation.

"Let's get going," I said, turning back to the cupcakes. "Get your sweater, boots, hat—"

"But it's not snowing!" Nick whined. The day outside was warm and clear, strange for the end of December.

"It will!" I said.

"It won't!" he said.

"Oh yeah, Smartypants?" I said. "How do *you* know?"

And he said, "It's not going to snow till Daddy comes."

There are words that can kill you if you're not careful. "What did you say?" I asked, and he said it again, assuredly, as though this were scientific fact. Caterpillars metamorphosize and there's a butterfly. Egg fertilizes and there's a baby. Fathers return and there's snow. "Not till Daddy comes," he said. Then he picked up his backpack and ran out the door, leaving me to wonder what I'd say when the snow came and the daddy didn't.

Initially, meteorologists called it a fluke. No one much minded: no snow meant no shoveling, no bitter winds, no staggering gas bills; but when spring arrived without a snowfall, scientists kicked into gear. There were speculations, action plans; they spoke of increased environmental risks: tsunami, hurricanes, national crisis. Nick and I decorated our synthetic Christmas tree and went on with our lives: work and school and growing up. By the time he turned eighteen, snow was more of a memory, like an extinct species. You see photographs in encyclopedias, but you've learned to live without it.

Until today.

From the window, I watched Nick run shirtless into the front yard and make angels in the snow, his body a straight line, then an X. At first it fell gently, delicate flakes dancing in the air, but soon the sky turned electric white and the wind whipped with increasing violence. Two inches layered on the windowsill and it didn't take long for that to double. Double again. I grabbed clothes for Nick and an afghan for me, then went out to the porch.

"Mom, it's *snow!*" Nick cried, almost buried, his bare chest red against the white.

"I know, baby. Put these on," I said. The snow came up to his calves and he forged a path toward me. As he dressed, he talked excitedly about this moment, his first remembered snowfall. There's a kind of joy in watching someone experience a thing for the first time. I thought of my own firsts: first kiss, first paycheck, first time I saw my son.

"I'm going to the park," Nick said, and I pulled out of my head and looked at him. My boy, the red hat pulled down over his ears, blue eyes shocking under its rim. His chest pushed at the knitting of his sweater. His jaw was strong and square. He was grown, and this was another first: first time ever in my own life. What would I do first?

"Have fun, Nick," I said, and he took off, struggling to open the front gate almost buried under a snowdrift, then giving up and vaulting over it. I watched him disappear into the white, his red hat bobbing as he ran toward the park. Out in the street, people held their palms to the sky, needing to touch it to believe it, verifiable proof of this wholly impossible thing, and that's when I saw another red hat coming from the other direction. It stopped at my gate, trying to push it open through the snow, and suddenly I didn't feel the cold. I didn't feel anything. There wasn't any room for feeling. There was only Joe, standing before me in the big empty hole my son had just vacated.

"Hi," he said.

That was it.

Hi.

Twelve years had passed and in my mind I'd played this scene a thousand different ways, but in that moment, none of them seemed right. I just sat there and looked: he hadn't changed at all, and everything about me felt new.

"Can I see Nick?" he asked.

"Not my call," I said. "Nick's his own man."

Joe's whole body reacted to the word *man*. It botched his fantasy of stepping back into our lives as if he'd only been gone a moment.

"He's at the park," I said.

Joe didn't move.

"He's changed a lot, but you'll recognize him," I said. "He looks like you."

Joe stood there, buried past his waist.

"Are you going to go find him?" I asked after a while.

"Yeah," he said. "I'm going," but he didn't.

I remembered my old fantasy: me and Joe and our kids at the pool, the perfect family smiling for the camera. Except if you look a little closer, maybe you'd see that the daughter's not happy; the man doesn't want to be there; and the woman's smile is pinched, frozen, forced.

Amazing what you see when you look a little deeper.

And Joe? He wasn't the person I wanted to be looking at.

"Go home," I told him, and then I waited for something to happen. Something huge—I'd earned it, goddammit—and now was the time. Now was the time for the sky to split, a line of yellow sun to slide through the white. I'd watch Joe leave for the last time, his red hat going, going, gone. The sky would widen. The wind would die, and what happened next was a movie on fast-forward: first the snow piled level with my porch, then the frame quick-changed to slush, then to water, then the water was climbing, higher, an ocean at my ankles and I stood up fast. You couldn't see cars anymore: all were underwater like sunken ships with people standing on the front hoods, people treading water, people floating on their backs, and still the water climbed, heated by the sun like a bathtub faucet turning left, and as it reached my knees I got an idea for what I wanted do first.

I went inside the house, up the stairs, and pulled down the trapdoor in the hallway ceiling, climbing its little ladder to the attic and out through the window to the roof. Down in my front yard, water climbed past the second floor, gentle waves lapping at the windows. I stood there, as high as I'd ever been, watching the flood across the city.

Years from now, when somebody asks where you were on this day, maybe you'll tell them about that flood. Maybe you'll talk about the blizzard in August, or how snowflakes taste like Italian ice—but for me? It was the time I took a deep breath, plugged my nose, and then—wrapping my arms around my knees as I took off in the air—I jumped.

Do You Want to Have Sex
with Alan and Chloe?

Years ago, on our first date, my husband and I went to Danny's—this hipster bar in Bucktown—and we totally got hit on by swingers! which is complicated, 'cause, see, if it's just you getting hit on you can accept or decline and be done with it, but when you're part of a couple, there needs to be a *discussion.* It's like buying curtains. You can't just get the microsuede, you've got to ask, *Honey, what do you think about the microsuede?* Same thing with swinging. You can't just say yes or no, you've got to say, *What do you think, honey? Do you want to have sex with Alan and Chloe?*

They're the swingers from Danny's: he's is in advertising, she's a massage therapist, they met hiking in Colorado and so on and so on. We talked for over an hour and not once did I have any idea they wanted in our pants—although I'm not sure if they wanted in my pants or my future husband's pants or if everybody would be in everybody's pants, I wasn't entirely clear how all that stuff worked so I looked it up on Wikipedia and ohmygod there are so many *options*! Like:

1. If Chloe and I get down and Alan and my husband watch, it's open swinging;
2. If Alan and I go to one room and my husband and Chloe another, it's closed swinging;
3. If I date Chloe while my husband and I are together, that's an open relationship, but—

4. If I'm in a relationship with my husband *and* Chloe then I'm polyamorous and—
5. If all *four* of us date and have sex and live together on a big commune it's polyfidelity.

—but Alan and Chloe didn't bring up any of that.

They talked about their new condo, their trip to Port Aransas, the new Will Ferrell movie—they *love* Will Ferrell—and then Chloe, this little brunette in head-to-toe Banana Republic, took a big ol' swig from her vodka tonic and said, "So, do you party?"

This is a question I've been asked numerous times over the past decade, always in relation to different coded things:

1. Do you smoke pot?
2. Do you do coke?
3. Do you like girls?
4. Do you take it up the ass?

—I can never keep up.

"Could you be more specific?" I asked, and Alan—total average Joe, this guy: jeans, T-shirt, Chuck Taylors—leaned forward and said, "What she means is . . . do you two swing?"

Philosophically, I'm all for open relationships: I know tons of people have them and they can be very successful what with everybody's needs being met every which way but *people*. There have *got* to be rules!

Here's what I'm thinking:

1. The two primary parties in the relationship need to be clear on what they're doing, as in: Are they going off and doing their own separate thing? Or bringing the thing home to do together? And is the thing in question just sex, or is love okay, too, in which case how far is too far and is there any crossing the line? And—
2. The third party needs to be okay with all of that.

These rules must be adhered to *at all times*. Any deviation may result in broken hearts and fucked-up friendships and all other variations of unpleasantness.

This is what happened to me.

I met Jen back when I was a cocktail waitress at this swanky bar in the Gold Coast. She was the bartender, and at the end of my first shift she put a bourbon in my hands and invited me out dancing. I was twenty-one years old—I only drank Amaretto Stone Sours. "No thank you," I told her, "I've got homework," and I slid the drink back across the bar.

As far as friends go, Jen was totally out of my league: older and independent and super sexy. In fact she'd been a pole dancer for a while at Crazy Horse—I think that place is called VIPs, now, right? Guys? Have any of you been to VIPs? Anyhow, Jen slid the bourbon back across the bar, either not noticing or not caring that she intimidated the hell out of me. "Homework can wait," she said. "You should try something new for once."

I tried a lot of new things with Jen:

1. Bourbon
2. Pole dancing
3. Foam parties
4. Soft drugs
5. Other miscellaneous risk-taking that stopped just short of dangerous but still shoved me into life.

Man, I needed that shove—facing my fears, trying new things, having fun. We've all had a friend like that, right? And eventually the friend becomes our friend/roommate so the fun can keep going 24/7 while also splitting expenses because let's face it, fun ain't cheap, and Jen and I were having a *lot* of fun.

Until—

So many stories end this way—

She got a boyfriend.

Matthew.

Of whom you should understand three things:

1. He'd been an Ambercrombie and Fitch model, you know those guys? With the . . . *chests.*
2. He'd grown up in a nudist colony—and I know I make a lot of shit up for these stories but that's the God's honest truth—the man grew up on the Ponderosa Sun Club nudist colony in

Roselawn, Indiana. Feel free to Google it if you're eighteen and over. My point is the guy was very, very comfortable being naked. Like, all the time. And it's really difficult to *not* look at a penis when the penis is always there—*penis in the living room penis in the hall penis in the kitchen*—and did I mention I hadn't had sex in over a year?

What was I talking about? Oh yes:

3. He hit on me. A lot. And not in a subtle way, this was no "Heeeey, what's up?" that I could write off like *Oh, that's just Matthew being nice, hahaha, no*—the man would sit next to me on the couch totally naked and say, "We should have sex," the same way you might say, "We should make popcorn"—and *yes*, what I should've done is turn to him and say, "Matthew, that's completely inappropriate," and for the record I *did* do the whole turning to him part . . . which was far as I ever got 'cause *there was the penis* and it was . . . you know, *a penis*, and what do you *do* with that?! It's a steak in front of a starving woman!

So I went to my friend/roommate. "Jen, can we . . . talk?"

"Sure," she said. She was cutting limes for margaritas. "What's up?"

What I imagined in that moment was something straight out of *The Young and the Restless*: "I don't know how to tell you this," I'd say—we'd both have lots of jewelry and really big hair—"but Matthew—" "Stop right there," she'd cry, covering her eyes with the back of her hand—"I've known it all along!" Then she'd slap me, kill my child, drive off a cliff, and come back five years later with amnesia. Instead, she just reached for another lime and said, "And?"

"*And?*" I repeated. "I tell you your boyfriend hit on me and you say *and?*"

"It's not a big deal," she said, and then she put her limes in the blender, poured in tequila, and said, "We swing."

At the time, I had no idea what she was talking about. I was imagining, quite literally, the act of swinging on swings—as done by small children on the playground. Not the complicated-looking contraption sold at The Pleasure Chest that you bolt to your ceiling.

"It means," Jen explained patiently, "Matthew finds women for us to have sex with together."

My twenty-one-year-old self was not equipped for such things. I'd only had sex with one other person, how was I supposed to wrap my brain around three people *plus*? "And you . . . like that?" I asked.

"Sure."

"You like girls?"

"Sometimes," she said.

"Do you like me?"

And she said, "Yes."

We stared at each other.

Have you ever had a moment like that with a friend? They say they're into you or you say you're into them and what happens next is decided with a single look. I thought of all the things she'd showed me, and maybe I did need to be more open, and we did love each other, and as all those thoughts electrified the empty space between us, Matthew and his penis walked into the kitchen and said, "So what are we all talking about in here?"

Here's how I prepared for my very first three-way:

1. I went shopping at the Midwest equivalent of Fredrick's of Hollywood. For future reference: don't ever try on lingerie the day before you go to bed with a nudist and a stripper.
2. I panicked. My only-ever boyfriend had suffered from that whole *is it in there / is it not* issue, therefore my sexual experience was . . . not much, so—
3. I studied. Does anyone still watch Skinemax? If you haven't had the pleasure, Skinemax is a late-night soft porn channel with lots of nurses and secretaries accidentally falling out of their clothes in the janitor's closet—it's basically Cliff's Notes for a ménage à trois; however, you do foster some rather—shall we say—*unrealistic* expectations. I pictured Jen, for some reason, dressed as a cat with the fuzzy leotard and fishnets; Matthew, a naked pirate; I'm the German milkmaid and we're having sex in this anti-gravity chamber so we're like floating in midair—it was *awesome*.

But it didn't happen like that. It happened like this:

The three of us were in Jen's bed, our bodies wrapped together like a giant pretzel. It was dark. I couldn't tell whose leg that was? Whose fingers were those? What was I grabbing? Mentally, I now compare this experience to a step aerobics class—*Lift here! Arms there! Thrust this!*—you're sweaty and self-conscious but you gotta keep moving or else you'll fall behind! It was seriously about as far from sexy as you could get and, yes, I know a lot of it was my fault: I was young and awkward and just *thinking* too much. I remember wishing I could turn off my brain so my clitoris could do its thing without being interrupted with all this goddamn contemplation. Contemplation was not *fun!* and that's what I wanted: every other new thing I'd tried with Jen had been so exciting, and this, here—

We didn't look at each other. Not once.

After everybody came—or whatever the case may have been—I went back to my room. The next day, Jen and I didn't talk about it. It was like it hadn't happened.

Until a week later when it happened again.

Quick show of hands—who's gone to bed with someone you know you shouldn't be going to bed with? Why the fuck do we do that? Are we lonely? Are we masochists? I went to bed with Jen and Matthew for nearly three months—we lived together and slept together and grocery shopped together and argued about bills together—and I cannot tell you why. It wasn't fun, we didn't better ourselves as human beings, and we certainly didn't grow closer together; in fact, I moved out when the lease was up and . . . everything just stopped. The relationship, the friendship, all of it. I heard that not long after, Jen and Matthew broke up and she moved to Cincinnati to wait tables.

That was ten years ago, and as far as I know she's still there.

"That's the most *depressing* three-way story I've *ever heard*," my husband said when I first told him all this. We'd excused ourselves from Alan and Chloe and were sitting at the bar, having that inevitable *This is what I'm cool with / this is what I'm not cool with* conversation—you know the one I mean? The one that goes:

1. I'm not cool with being peed on; or
2. I'm not cool with whips and chains; or
3. I'm not cool with oral sex or sex on your period or sex in your mother's house (in which case I'd say, *dump him*, girls, 'cause that's just so, I don't know—Catholic?)

What I said to my husband was, "I'm not cool with open relationships."

"Good," he said, "me neither," and then he told me some stuff which—I can't even touch that, he'd *kill* me—*anyhow*, the point is: we were on the same page. That's what it's about, right? Whether you're polyamorous or monogamous or living on a commune, you've got somebody or many bodies that give you what you need. So when we went back to Alan and Chloe, we were all, "No, we won't be partying, thanks, but tell us again about Port Aransas!" and it wasn't weird or awkward. The four of us kept talking and had a few more drinks, and then they left to go do what they do and we left to do what we do.

And if you think I'm going to tell you what that is, you people are fucking crazy.

I Am the Keymaster

Here's the thing: I make nine dollars an hour copying keys at Ace Hardware. That's a thousand a month after taxes. Subtract whatever for bills and there's not much left for extras, let alone emergencies. Say your transmission falls out, or you need a root canal, or, in my case, you get in trouble—female trouble—and it costs four hundred bucks to fix even at Planned Parenthood which is supposed to be all cost-effective but I'm not some CEO or one of those Hilton sisters who can just charge their way out of a mistake. I mean, I save coupons. I go to Supercuts. I shop off Craigslist.

Stuff I Got off Craigslist
1. Dining room table $40
2. Five-dollar CTA card $4.50
3. Unopened twenty-pack Colgate $14
4. Bluebird paperweight, 10 cents. Not like I needed a paperweight, but *ten cents?* I earn that in less than one minute on the clock. You can't pass that up! I carry it in my pocket and grip it when I think I'm losing my mind.
5. Size 10 lady's whole closet, *free*. I guess she died—leukemia—and her husband couldn't handle it. *Please take ASAP*, said the post. *I don't want to remember anymore.* She liked the fancy stuff, this lady. I got a cashmere trench coat that goes all the way to the floor. Sometimes, when it's slow at work, I imagine millions of keys lining the inside of that coat. I imagine riding the El and suddenly it screeches to a stop and all the lights go off. Something terrible

71

is about to happen, we'll be exploded by a meteor or beheaded by terrorists or something, and everyone is screaming and banging on the doors but I remain calm. I reach into my trench coat. I pull out a key. It glows softly in the dark and people back away in awe—"Look, Mommy, we're saved!" cries a small, freckled child—as I unlock the locked door and lead everyone to safety. Sounds ridiculous, I know, but when you spend forty hours a week doing the same thing—find the key code, line up the keys, grind—you're really spending forty hours in your mind. Forty hours *thinking*, and in my case it's better to imagine impossible stuff than replay reality, 'cause, I'll tell you what, the reality is sort of shitty.

The reality is Dale, still wearing his Pep Boys uniform, sitting across from me at our Craigslist dining room table. His right leg bounces like it does when he's nervous. "How can you be pregnant?" he asks.

I think of that video from sixth-grade biology with the cartoon sperm narrating how babies are made. "I don't know," I say, reaching into my pocket, grabbing the bluebird, squeezing it so tight the beak cuts into my palm.

Dale's knee bangs into the underside of the table. "Was it that time the condom—?" he stops before the word *broke*. "Or when we—?" *drank too much.* "Or—" *Pulled out, too fast, in the backseat, weren't thinking, stupid stupid stupid kids.*

"Dale," I interrupt, because we're supposed to be making a decision.

Except it's already made.

"He told you *what*?" said my sister Adelle. She goes to community college and is right now taking a Womyn's Studies Class. Womyn with a Y.

"To get rid of it," I said.

"And what did you say?"

"Nothing," I said, which got her all sorts of worked up. She talked like there was a whole press corps in her living room. "When are you going to stand up for yourself? When are you going to face these years of oppression and say to them, 'Years, I will not be held back! This is the twenty-first century and I can, nay I *will* do it all! I will work my job and feed my young and wear a skirt while doing so because—'"

"I don't even know what you're talking about," I told her, so she got off her fake pedestal and asked what I was going to do.

"I already did it," I said. That's when I started to cry. Saying it aloud made me remember—last week, the waiting room, the paper robe, the *You'll feel some discomfort*—so I tried to think about something else. Adelle has this big fireplace and I imagined that inside it was a door. I go to it, and then I reach inside my coat and pull out a key and unlock the door and stretching out before me is a whole starry universe and all I have to do is walk through and I'll be somewhere else. Somewhere away.

Adelle patted my shoulder. "You need to protect yourself," she said. "In case this happens again."

Starry universe, starry universe, I thought, rubbing the bluebird with my thumb.

"You should really go on the pill."

I don't have fifty bucks a month for the pill. I have rent and gas and electric and phone and school loans from that one semester before I dropped out and health insurance out-of-pocket and that loan from when I got my wisdom teeth out and the loan from when our mom died and the funeral, and my car and car insurance and groceries and beer and cat food and cat litter and the vet bill from when the cat ate a lightbulb and and and—

So I did like I did with the dining room table.

PILL 4 SALE CHEAP

Reply to: loopdloo@yahoo
 My insurance thinks I have a uterine bleeding problem so I pay ten dollars for Ortho Tri-Cyclen. My husband and I don't need it because he got a vasectomy. We need money we are saving for a new deck. Will sell twenty dollars per.

Here's the email I got back:

The Beachwood, Sunday night, 10 p.m. I have red hair.

I know. It's shady as all hell.

But you've got to understand: I couldn't let it happen again.

The Beachwood is a bar over by the Jewel. It's a dive for sure, all dark, peeling plaster and neon signs. Dale and I went there sometimes 'cause the beers were cheap, but I never saw any other customers. The bartender was over sixty, with red lipstick colored outside the lines. She never said a word, just held up fingers for however many dollars we owed her. Dale would watch TV and I'd imagine pulling a key out of my coat and leaning across the bar. I insert it between the bartender's red red lips and suddenly she starts talking, same as those dolls that need their strings pulled.

"Can I ask you something?" she says, her voice two-packs-a-day, easily.

"Sure," I say.

"What'cha doing with this goof?" She nods her head at Dale, who's lost in whatever's on. We haven't spoken in hours. We haven't spoken in months and I am alone in an empty bar.

But *that* night, it's not empty. *That* night, 10:00 p.m. on Sunday, I went to the Beachwood and could barely squeeze in it was so packed. I wondered if it was a bachelorette party, or a protest, 'cause everybody in there was a woman.

"Is Sleater-Kinney playing or something?" I asked the lady pressed in to my right. She had green hair and a tattoo on her neck.

"I don't know," she said. "I'm here for the pill."

"Me, too," said the girl to my left. "You see any redheads?"

"Hang on," I said. "Is everybody here for the pill?"

Lots of people heard that question, even over "Smooth Criminal" on the jukebox. A chorus of *Yeah's* and *I am's!* came from all around me. The soccer moms in capri pants. The college students, sweatshirts emblazoned in Greek. The teenagers, wide-eyed, watching their backs—and from there the voices erupted.

"Who's gonna get it?"

"Me, I need it!"

"Everybody needs it!"

"Where's the redhead?"

They got louder, girls all up in each other's faces, heads whipping from shoulder to shoulder like *That's my Ortho-Tri-fucking-Cyclen* and I thought of movie scenes where the crowd panics and tramples itself to death. In the midst of it all, a woman stood on the bar and yelled,

"Everybody, listen!" She wore a business suit, the skirt high on her thighs from climbing. Women like her come into Ace Hardware for do-it-yourself catalogues. "Is the person who posted on Craigslist here?" The group went quiet. Everyone looked around.

"Okay," said the woman after a few seconds. "We got screwed. We should all go home and—"

"Fuck that!" yelled somebody in the crowd. "We came for the pill and we're leaving with the pill!"

Everybody cheered; somebody yelled, "How?"

"There's a clinic right up the street!" yelled somebody else. "They've got tons of samples!"

It was well past midnight by that point, so maybe a couple hours of drinking had done its job. Maybe it was that freak mob-mentality you see on the news. Or maybe all the women in that bar had a story like mine, one we were trying to forget. Whatever the reason, we moved as one through the street that night. Old and young, ugly and beautiful and scarred. I was near the front of the crowd, close enough to hear the girl who first reached the clinic door yell out what we all must have known anyway: "It's *locked*!"

I know. What I *should've* done was walk away, but what I *did* do was walk forward toward that door. In my head, I'd pictured this moment a thousand times: I open a stylish trench coat and the inside is lined with keys, all identical-looking, and I grab one of them—to the untrained eye it would seem random but me? I know. I am the Keymaster, the Asian guy in the second *Matrix*, I can unlock a goddamn dimension if I have to! I take the key and put it in the lock and lead us into that clinic. I have another key to open the cabinets, and hundreds and hundreds of free samples rain onto the floor and we pack them into backpacks and rush off through the night, thrusting the little plastic cases into the hands of women on the way. I got so excited in that fantasy that I forgot the truth of it all: the math and the broken condom and the fifty dollars a month, all these girls showing up in some bar and me with my imagination.

I didn't have any keys. But I did have that bluebird, heavy and pulsing in my pocket, and I slammed it against the clinic's front window. The glass cracked into a giant spiderweb and as I watched it go I thought, *I will not be held back!*

75

This Teacher Talks Too Fast

When I first started teaching, I thought it would go like *Dead Poets Society*: we'd rip up our textbooks, quote Whitman, play soccer to opera music, and if ever anyone was in trouble I'd know just how to save them.

That was a decade ago, and I've gotten more realistic. College textbooks are expensive, there's no way we'd rip them up; and my students don't listen to opera, they listen to emo; and I can't save anybody. I teach creative writing—voice, structure, point of view; none of that's going to help Rachel who's pregnant or Kyle with the antidepressants or Dennis who's *way* more interested in pot than he is in class, and I have these days sometimes where it's like, what the hell am I doing? This past semester was especially rough and on the last day, as I was packing my things for winter break, I thought, *I could walk away.*

What if I walked away?

On the way out, I grabbed my mail—memos, a stack of student work, and a book. I checked the cover—some lit journal from a community college—and was all set to toss it when I noticed a page was marked with a Post-it Note. I opened it to a short story, saw the name of the author, and stopped.

Okay. In order to explain what happened next, I need you to imagine that I'm a character on *Grey's Anatomy*. I'm thinking specifically of the episode where Izzie gives up being a doctor—she's got eight million dollars from her dead fiancé and she goes to say goodbye to Dr. Burke who first taught her how to do a running whipstitch and she tells him, "I'm sorry," 'cause it's her fault he got shot and has a tremor in his hand and maybe can't be a surgeon anymore and he says, "Don't you be sorry because of me. You have two good hands and you're not using them, be sorry for that!" At this point, some pop song by a new up-and-coming artist starts playing and Izzie's face jerks as though she's been slapped. She stands there, confused and frozen in Burke's office until slowly, slowly, she looks down at her hands, holding them in front of her like she's about to play the piano. She studies every finger, every wrinkle, and turns them so the palms face upward. We stare at those hands, all of us, imaging the thousands of lives they might save, and the camera pans back to Izzie's face, her lovely blue eyes wide and determined. *My God, what am I doing?* she thinks. *How can I give up becoming a surgeon?* And then, the song crescendos or maybe changes chord in some significant way and—she smiles. It all becomes clear. She's not going to quit! She's going to stay and be a great doctor! And here, here is the important part: it might never have happened if it hadn't been for Burke.

Just like that lit journal in my mailbox means nothing unless I tell you about Andrew.

It was my second year of teaching. I was twenty-three and still naive enough to think we could all recite Whitman standing on our desks—except we don't have desks in the Fiction Writing Department at Columbia College, we sit in semicircles so you can look everyone in the eye. It was the first day of class and I was calling out attendance.

"Elizabeth?"

"Here."

"Angela?"

"Here."

"Andrew—?"

"Andrew—?"

I looked up. "Andrew—?" and I will never forget this; he said, "I'm fuckin' here already." This guy was nineteen, South Side Irish Catholic complete with the accent, very baggy jeans belted just below his crotch and these giant headphones that he would not turn off unless you told him to, like, "Andrew, we're starting class, can you lose the Eminem please?"

"Whatever," he'd say, which was all he ever said.

"Whatever," when we talked about Baldwin.

"Whatever," when we discussed student work.

"Whatever," when I told him he was failing. It was the fifth week of classes and he'd missed three already. When he did show it was an hour late, headphones blaring, sitting in the back of the room a good ten feet away from the rest of us in our semicircle, and it's very, very difficult to continue reading Faulkner under those circumstances. Had I been the teacher I am now, I'd have told Andrew he could join us after the break, but then? I wanted to save everybody.

"So if you don't care about failing," I asked, "why are you still coming to class?"

Andrew's hair hung past his nose—I wanted to tell him to move it so I could look him in the eye. "My mom'll freak out if I don't," he said.

"This is college," I said. "Your mother doesn't—"

"Look, I fuckin' paid for the class," he said. "I'm fuckin' gonna come to it." In that moment I was afraid of Andrew—not that I thought he'd hurt me physically, but that maybe he could tell I didn't have a clue what I was doing.

"Fine," I said. "But you have to write. We're a third of the way through the semester and you haven't given me any writing and—"

While I was talking, he stood up and opened his backpack, taking out a couple typed pages and dropping them in my lap.

Then he was gone.

His writing was really, really good, and it was about a guy who wanted to kill himself. Now, lots of students write about suicide, but for some reason this felt different. It didn't feel like fiction. Usually, in such situations, you've got three options:

1 Ignore it, which really isn't an option so far as I'm concerned so—
2. Contact somebody who knows what they're doing. I called the college's counseling hotline—and, for the record, I felt like a total asshole, like I was ratting out this guy's creative work, but me being an asshole was better than him being dead. Turns out, there's all sorts of legal implications to this stuff. This is college. Andrew is an adult—he has to choose to seek out counseling. I could suggest it but not enforce it, which brings me to—
3. Talk to Andrew directly.

Halfway through the semester, we do one-on-one conferences with every student—an hour-long sit-down to go over the strongest elements in their work. These are held in closet-sized cubicles in a hallway off the Fiction Office, which is good because of the privacy but also a little unnerving. Picture you and a semi-stranger locked up in a bathroom for an hour. Now picture Andrew and me during his conference, the two of us in this tiny, cramped space and I'm making suggestions for his writing, like, "Could you maybe slow down the scene? Right here, when the character is taking all those pills and drinking all the vodka?" because that's my job, right? To focus on his work? And then say something very subtle that'll inspire him to seek help on his own? Well, it is *not, not, not* that simple because sometimes those perfect words get all stuck in your throat and you end up saying the absolute worst thing possible, like: "*So.* How're you *doing?*"

"Fine," he said.

"Fine?" I said. "Like, really fine?"

I couldn't see his eyes through the hair, but I knew he was looking at me like I was nuts. "Okay," I said. "Look. Do you need to . . . talk to somebody? I mean, there are people here who—" Just like last time, he was on his feet and packing up. "Andrew!" I said. I wanted to reach out and grab his arm but figured that touching him would be as far from appropriate as I could get. "I'm just trying to help!"

He turned and faced me then. "It's *fiction*," he said. "Isn't that what this is? A fuckin' *fiction* class?" and then he was gone.

I sat there in the cubicle for a really long time. I don't remember my exact train of thought, but it went something like *why can't I get through to him, how do I reach him, how do I save him.* I didn't know then what I do now: his life was so much bigger than my little one class a week. Think back for a second to when you were a freshman in college. What were you the most focused on? Me? My folks were splitting up, my boyfriend back in Michigan was seeing somebody else, and I shared a twelve-by-twelve-foot dorm room with a girl looped on ecstasy four nights outta the week, I tell you what, teachers were the *last* thing on my mind.

My job is to help their writing, not save their lives.

Right?

I gave Andrew an F, and on the last day of class I asked him to stay after. "You failed to fulfill the standards and policies of this class," I told him. "It doesn't mean that you're not a good writer."

"Whatever," he said. "I'm done with this school bullshit anyhow—" and then, like always, he was gone.

At the end of every semester, teachers turn in grades and all copies of student work to the Fiction Office, at which time we're given our student evaluations. I flipped through the stack and found one that hadn't been filled out except for a single line in Andrew's handwriting. It said: *I can't smoke pot before this class. This teacher talks too fast.*

I thumbtacked that evaluation to my wall and looked at it for a while. Then, I put it in a box under my bed. *Shake it off*, I told myself. *New students, new chapter.* The first day of the spring semester I walked into class, called out attendance.

"Kelly?"

"Here."

"LaTasha?"

"Here."

"Brian—?"

"Brian—?"

"*Brian—?*" I looked up and it was *total deja vu.* Same baggy pants, same headphones, same accent even! Except this wasn't Andrew. It wasn't Andrew. It was Brian, slouching in his seat and looking at me like *All right, sweetheart. What are you gonna do for me?*

He didn't show up the second week of class.

He didn't show up the third week.

On the fourth week he rolled in an hour late and sat down in the back of the room. That's when I sort of lost my mind. "All right, out in the hall," I told him. "Everybody else—read something, or something." As I left the classroom, I tried to calm down. *This is not Andrew*, I told myself. *Don't put Andrew on this guy.*

"I'm sorry," he said, moving the hair out of his face. He had blue eyes. "The past couple weeks have been a nightmare."

"I'm sorry," I said. "But that doesn't excuse—"

"My friend killed himself," he said. "It's not your problem, I know, I just told you so you don't think I'm slacking off."

I said I'd help him catch up after class.

"Thank you," he said. "But actually, my friend? He was a student here. And I know they've got some of his work in the office and I was wondering if you could get it for me. I know he wouldn't want his parents to see it."

I said something about the legality of the situation, how I'd have to ask the chair of my department, and did he know the name of his friend's teacher so I could speak to them directly?

And he said—"It was you. You were Andrew's teacher."

In class I tell my students there are words for every emotion and it's our challenge as writers to find them. I have tried over and over to explain how I felt in that moment and *every* time I fail. I can tell about the guilt, about how part of me, the idealistic part, died right then and there. I can tell you how horrible it was but I won't even come close. "Excuse me," I said to Brian. Then I went into the office and down the hall, locked myself into a conference cubicle and cried. It was the first time I'd ever done that, and it certainly hasn't been the last.

My colleagues were really wonderful, and I might not have gotten through it without their support and advice. "Do the best you can," they told me. "Focus on the students you have now."

For me, that meant Brian.

He came to class sporadically, but when he did he was really involved and even, I think, had a good time. He told about growing up on the South Side, specifically a series of stories about the Catholic school he and Andrew attended when they were kids. I don't know if it was therapeutic for him to write about Andrew, but it sure was for me to read it.

In the end, I gave him a C, and on the last day of class I asked him to stay after. "You got a C 'cause you weren't here half the time," I told him. "It doesn't mean you're not a good writer."

He smiled, sliding those giant headphones over his ears. "School's never been my thing," he said. "And this place costs too much anyway." He made it halfway through the door before he turned back around. "You know, Andrew told me to take your class," he said.

I waited. What I wanted to hear was, *He said you really helped him*, or *He said you were inspiring*, or *He said you almost saved him*.

What I heard instead was, "He said you were . . . interesting."

That was ten years ago. Twenty semesters. Multiply that times three classes at two schools equals—more than *seven hundred* students I've worked with over the years and, through all of it, the names and faces and page upon page of writing, I have never once forgotten Brian.

So picture it: I'm standing in front of my faculty mailbox, getting ready to walk out the door for winter break or maybe a hell of a lot longer, and I find this book, some lit magazine from a community college, and when I open it, there's Brian's name on the top of the page. I stare at it for a while, remembering him and Andrew and how I once thought I could save the world, and then I read the story; it's about how Brian got kicked out of Catholic school for calling a nun a whore. "What are you going to do with your life?" his mother asks as they walk to the car. "What are you going to *do*?" I remember when he first told it, ten years ago in my class, the week after his best friend's funeral—and that's when I get it: my job is not just story structure and point of view and imagery. It's Brian putting that book in my mailbox. It's Chris calling the night before he shipped out to Iraq. It's Rudy writing from prison and Kate getting a Fulbright and Byron starting his own magazine. I imagine a camera closing in on my face then; my eyes are wide and determined. *My God, what am I doing?* I think. *How can I give up being a teacher?*

At the very least, I'll always be interesting.

I Asked the Guy Why Are You So Fly

"Thirty is the new twenty," Bridget told me on my thirtieth birthday. We were having brunch at one of those very hip places, with honeydew mimosas and servers who are really fashion models. Makes you wonder, how do they not spill honeydew mimosas all over their expensive designer clothes? Why do they wear expensive designer clothes to serve breakfast? Why do people wear expensive designer clothes to *eat* breakfast? Even Bridget had on an electric-pink Juicy jumpsuit. And a spray tan. Which made her look orange. Pink and orange. Which is maybe the new black, like thirty being the new twenty. Bridget turned thirty a couple months ago and since then she's developed a few—how should I say this?—*quirks.* The spray tanning, for one. A particular fondness for the word "asshat" (as in, "Of *course* we're having brunch on your birthday, Diane, don't be an asshat!"). The valley girl accent is another. She sounds like Julie in the movie *Valley Girl*: *Encino is, like so bitchin'! Twenty is, like, the new thirty!* which apparently Bridget found comforting, but not me. I was in nooo hurry to replay my twenties: The indecision. The self-loathing. The dating.

"Are you dating?" my mother always asked.

"Yes," I'd say. We had this conversation so many times it could've been scripted.

HER: Anyone special?

ME: No.

HER: You're almost thirty!

ME: Insert long soliloquy about this being the twenty-first century, didn't she read Gloria Steinem? I have a good job, good friends, it's like the Destiny's Child song that goes *Don't need no man, I bought this rock I'm rockin' blah blah* but the truth was, I knew why I wasn't with anyone special.

Take my last date. While he talked about camping in Wisconsin, I made a list on my napkin.

How This Guy and the Last Five Guys I've Gone Out with Are Exactly the Same
1. They camp in Wisconsin.
2. They listen to the Foo Fighters.
3. They drink imported beer.
4. They have complex relationships with their mothers.
5. They have responsible corporate jobs.
6. I had sex with all of them (about which I could write a whole other sub-list titled *How This Guy and the Last Five Guys I've Had Sex with Have Sex in Exactly the Same Way*).

"Happy birthday!" Bridget said. She ordered two more mimosas from Kate Moss and handed me a card. On the front were tiny pictures of different men, each about an inch wide so several could fit onto the paper. Over them was printed: *For your birthday, I wanted to get you thirty hot guys!* I opened the card and read: *So I DID!* and beneath it, in smaller writing: *Fastdater, Incorporated.*

Bridget was smiling, waiting for me to rush over and hug her. In our twenties, she and I hadn't been the hugging kind of friends, but now we were in our thirties, which were the new twenties, and I was supposed to hug and wear shimmery lip gloss and know what Fastdater, Incorporated, was.

"So I got the idea 'cause I was dating Lance who was a total asshat and this girl I work with Stephanie said *Come with me speed dating!* and I went and was like WOW and I know how shitty it is to turn thirty and be alone but this is so much fun!" and then she jumped up, ran over, and hugged me. She smelled like the entire Marshall Field's counter, and I wondered how a number—a three and a zero—could turn my seemingly normal friend into this orange huggy thing. Would it happen to me? Come midnight, would I also turn into a pumpkin?

"Bridget," I said into her hair, "what exactly is speed dating?"

"This is how it works," said Tina. She was addressing the sixty Fastdater customers crowded into Leopard Lounge, a dark, smoky bar with—surprise!—leopard-spotted upholstery. The candle-lit tables had been lined up in rows around the room, each with two chairs and a number, one through thirty. "Everyone has a badge," said Tina. Hers said *Hi, my name is Tina*. Mine said *#12*. "You'll meet your first date at the table that corresponds with your number, and you'll have three minutes until I ring this bell." She demonstrated: *ping ping*. "Then, women stay seated and guys move one table over, again and again till everybody's met everybody. Everybody ready?"

Initially, I wasn't going to do it. But since my birthday, everything had sucked. Not because something had happened; because *nothing* had happened.

How Every Day Since I Turned Thirty Has Been Exactly the Same
1. Traffic sucks
2. Edit copy
3. Corner Bakery / chopped salad
4. Edit more copy
5. Lean Cuisine / America's Next Top Model
6. Can't sleep / Sominex, an over-the-counter sleeping pill that knocks you out, but keeps you in this perpetual half-sleep stage. You move slowly. Colors are dull. In conversation, the other person says *murp murp mrrrruuuup*.

I needed something to wake me up, a bowl of ice water in my face. So far, Fastdating was doing the trick: The Techicolor leopard print. The vodka tonics. The overwhelming possibility.

I sat at table #12 across from a good-looking guy in his mid-thirties; expensive suit, bourbon on ice. *Nice*, I thought. *He's got all his hair.*

ping ping

"Bruce/divorced/tax attorney/scuba," he said, all one word. "What's your lead?"

"My what?"

"Lead, lead, you've got to have a lead-in question, like *What's your favorite book? What music do you listen to? Do you like sushi?*, whatever, something to jumpstart conversation or else you're going to waste our whole three minutes."

"How many times have you done this?" I asked.

"A few. Look, we've pissed away a full minute already. You got a lead yet?"

"Uhm—"

"Let's GO!"

"Uhm—What's your favorite book?"

He groaned, like I'd asked the stupidest thing in the entire universe, and then talked nonstop about *The Seven Effective Habits of Whoever* until the bell rang. On the table in front of us were pencils and paper. He grabbed them and started writing.

"What are you doing?" I asked.

He groaned again. "You write what you think of the date next to their number. When tonight is over, you enter the numbers you like on Fastdater's website, and if we both entered each other, then we go out for real."

"Oh," I said, taking paper and pencil. Next to #12 I wrote: *Asshat.*

ping ping

#11—tall, stubble, polo shirt—sat down across from me and extended his hand. "Eddie," he said. "I'm a copywriter."

"Me too!" I said. We shook.

"What music do you listen to?" he asked. "I like the Foo Fighters."

Next to #11, I wrote: *He likes the Foo Fighters.*

ping ping

"Hi," said #10. "I'm James. What music do you listen to?"

#10, I wrote. *Also Foo Fighters.*

ping ping

#9: *Foo Fighters.*

#8: *Foo Fighters.*

#7, 6, 5—

ping ping

"Isn't this weird?" said #4. "Meeting people like this?"

"I know!" I said.

"My brothers got me a gift certificate," he said. "They thought I needed to get out more."

"My friend bought one for me!" I said. This was looking up. I checked him out: older, past forty maybe; in good shape, like he had a personal trainer. "It was a birthday present," I told him.

"Yeah?" he said. 'Which birthday?"

"The big one," I said. "Thirty."

"Oh," he said. "I don't date women over twenty-five. "Too much commitment."

#4, I wrote: *Asshat.*

ping ping

"My favorite book?" said #3. "The Harry Potters. I think she's developing a global community and—"

ping ping

"*A Million Little Pieces.* I'm an addict myself and—"

ping ping

"My favorite book? Why, the Bible of cour—"

ping ping

"Nice to meet you," said #30. He was very thin, in a suit and fuzzy winter hat. We talked for a while and it was good. *I could see this guy again!* I thought, and he said, "I should tell you I have cancer."

Oh.

"I was diagnosed a couple months ago."

Ohhhhhh.

"I have a hard time talking about it, so I do speed dating to practice. You can say anything to a stranger, you know."

ping ping

At that point, I was done. This was ridiculous, it was bullshit. *Me and my Sominex are outta here!* I thought, standing up to leave at the same time #29 sat down.

ping ping

This guy was—first—Black—and second—*big,* wearing a two-sizes-too-big baseball jersey and a backwards baseball cap. He had a thin stubble mustache over his upper lip, and around his neck were four or five thick chains with different things dangling from them. He was like no one I'd ever seen in person—this guy was a music video or an album cover—a total one-eighty from every guy who'd sat across a table from me.

"Hi," he said. His voice was deep and scratched. "I'm Tone."

"Hi, Tony," I said, sitting back down. "It's really dark in here, why are you wearing sunglasses?"

This guy leaned forward across the table and beckoned me closer. He spoke low, like he was telling a secret. "I don't want to be recognized," he said.

"Are you hiding out?" I asked, thinking *The feds?*

"No, baby! I got fans, you know, and I don't want to be bothered with all that right now."

"Okay then," I said. "What's your favorite bo—"

"Okay," he interrupted. "You really want to know who I am?"

I nodded, and he reached up and lowered his sunglasses so I could see his eyes. We stared at each other for a minute—me searching my memory, searching, searching, nothing—and he put the glasses back. "See?" he said.

I shook my head.

"Okay, okay, listen," he said, and he picked up a pencil and held it like a microphone: *"And we go a little something like this, hit it!"*

He sat back, giving me this look like *Uh-huh!*, but I still didn't know.

"Were you living in a barn in '89? Didn't have a radio in the house?"

"I was fourteen in '89," I told him. "I listened to Debbie Gibson."

He slumped back in his seat. Through the candlelight and the vodka, I thought he looked sad. I thought I could make him feel better. "Sing a little more," I said.

"Naw," he said. "I can't."

"Please!"

"Naw."

"Come on!" I said, and before I could even get the words out, this guy whipped a boom box out from underneath the table and pressed play.

As the bass and drums got going, he stepped first onto his chair and then the table. I was eye-level with his knees, his baggy denim and hiking boots stepping side-to-side with the music.

"Is that a cowbell?" I yelled up at him.

He looked down and grinned as a spotlight appeared out of nowhere and locked on him.

All around us, the Fastdaters stared. Some were embarrassed and looked at the floor. Some tried to continue their dates as though nothing was happening. Some scowled and others laughed, it was all so complete-ly ridiculous: Tone on the table; the three-minute dates; this relentless, sometimes desperate search for love. Still, we were all here. We'd always be here, because—if we're really being honest—is there anything more important?

That's when #30 stood up. Remember #30? The fuzzy hat? The cancer in his bones? He was just one table over so I had an excellent view: he moved his body, slowly, side-to-side. He lifted his arms, swirling them in front of him like he was treading water.

Dancing. He was dancing.

"What's he singing?" asked the girl next to me at table #11.

"Funky Comedina," said her date.

"What's a Comedina?" I asked.

"A medina is the oldest part of a North African city," #11 said, and, in answer to my look: "I'm a geography teacher. But I don't know what a Comedina is, maybe a—"

"*Cold* Medina," said her date. "Funky *Cold* Medina."

"Coming up," said the bartender.

"Excuse me," said the girl on my other side, #13. "I take issue with this song. He—" she gestured at Tone, dancing on the table— "is advocating the use of GHB, also known as the date rape drug. He slips this—" she put up her fingers in air quotes— " 'medina' into women's drinks in order to—" again with the air quotes— " 'get' them on their 'back.' "

For some reason, I felt the need to defend him. "The only ones drink-ing medina in the song are dogs and a lady named Sheena."

The bartender set shot glasses down on our table. "What's in them?" asked the guy at #11.

"Vodka, Southern Comfort, Blue Curacao, and cran," said the bartender.

"Here," I said to the girl at #13. "Have a shot. Loosen up." And then I did the shot.

And then I did another. And another, and everything became surpris-ingly clear.

"Everybody!" I called out. "Have a drink! Medinas all around!"

That was the beginning. By the end, we were all up and dancing: the asshats and the Foo Fighters, all the girls in lingerie tops and expensive jeans, one of us looking so much like the other. How can you really tell someone apart unless you know them? How can you know them in three little minutes?

It's impossible.

But I've lived thirty years, and it feels like I don't even know myself.

Greek or Czech or Japanese

There's this diner up the street called the Golden House. Total relic, this place: red vinyl seats, waitresses in aprons and support hose, and you'll get a contact high off the coffee whether you drink it or not. My husband and I used to eat there every Sunday—dragging ourselves up by noon so two eggs and bacon could soak up all the stupidity from the night before—but then I got pregnant and all I ate for four months was white rice and saltines, not to mention the smell of coffee made me want to stick a fork in my eye. Happily, that all goes away in the second trimester and last weekend I woke up with my very survival dependent on diner food. "I need biscuits and gravy," I told my husband, shaking him out of bed at seven-thirty. "And hobo hash and potato pancakes and Belgian waffles with peaches," which at the Golden House means a plate of Bisquick with canned peaches in syrup poured on top and if I didn't have it immediately the world might stop spinning from the sheer power of my brain so there we were, my wonderful husband nursing coffee on his only day off and me trying to keep from eating the individual butter packets I was so goddamned hungry. We sat in a booth by the window, front-row seats for people watching. A young couple walked up to the diner with a little kid, maybe two years old, yellow-haired and adorable and pushing his own stroller down the sidewalk, his parents smiling and laughing in their Pumas and their backpacks and their fun, hipster style. "This way, Dominick!" called the mom, holding out her arms—they were tattooed down to the wrists and the dad had ones that matched, all urban style and love and happy baby and I thought, *How do they make it look so easy?* I thought, *Give me a sign that I'll do okay.* I thought, *What kind of stroller is that, that's a really nice stroller, we'll need a stroller soon, won't we?*

In my early twenties, I'd walk down the street and watch guys. Later, after I met my husband, I'd watch for things to write about.

What I do these days is watch parents.

I'm trying to figure out how to be one.

Here's what I see: dads with backpack Baby Bjorns and moms with double-wide strollers, happy families picking out Halloween pumpkins and screaming children running unsupervised through brunch restaurants, women whacking their kids on the Red Line train home from work and dads on the news getting arrested for horrible things and in the middle of all this, people I don't know look at my stomach and ask what kind of diapers we'll use, will I stay home from work, will I Feberize, will I pump? "Pump what?" I said to the random woman who asked that, and she looked so shocked, like how dare I carry this child when I don't know the fundamentals of breast feeding and I wanted to say *How dare I? You better back the fuck up, lady, I have hormones coming out my EARS!* but I figured that wouldn't have been very maternal of me. So I smiled. Then I went home and read on the internet about pumping versus formula, natural birth versus epidural, baby registries and Montessori school and five-point harnesses and lead paint and 529 college savings plans and what will happen if I eat unpasteurized cheese. "There's so much information!" I said in the direction of my stomach. For the past month I've been imagining that we wear headsets—my kid and I—like FBI agents, or Madonna, so we can communicate even at a great distance. "I don't know what to do with all if it!" And he said, "Figure it out."

At the Golden House, Dominick and his parents took the booth right behind ours. The mom and I were back-to-back, and if my husband leaned in either direction he could look around me at the dad. I pretended to drop my fork so I could sneak a close-up: how the mom brought crayons to keep Dominick busy, how the dad tossed him in the air to make him laugh, how they settled him into a booster seat so easily, not worried at all that they might break him. I think about that sometimes—that I'll break the kid. That I won't know how to feed him, or I'll forget something important, or I won't be able to protect him from the enormity of this world, but then the food arrived, plate after plate on our table, and I forgot everything else: the fear, the questions, and Dominick's happy family, because there, in front of me, was bacon. And huevos rancheros. And syrup and cream cheese and French fuckin' toast. "The doctor says we don't need all of this," I told my kid. "The doctor says you only need 300 extra calories a day to grow." And he said, "Tell the doctor to suck it."

I found out I was pregnant in the women's bathroom at Uncommon Ground, this fancy coffee shop on the North Side. I was there to meet a friend for lunch, and on the way I'd had this feeling. It's tricky to describe—I wasn't nauseous, or achy, my period wasn't running late or anything, but for some reason I stopped at Walgreens and bought a two-pack Clearblue test. I'm sure lots of people have experienced this next part: sitting on the bathroom floor and waiting, waiting, waiting, trying not to look at your watch as the three minutes tick by between peeing on the stick and your whole life changing. I'd done this one time before, long ago in an Italian hotel, nineteen years old and scared out of my mind. *Please please please*, I'd repeated, hands clasped together and eyes shut tight. The guy was long gone and I was new to foxhole religion. *Please please please*. This time, I was thirty-one; good job, money in the bank, and a husband I was so crazy about I could hardly breathe sometimes. *Please please please*, I said, but this time my eyes were wide open and the words meant something different. Seconds ticked by and my heart beat fast and I wanted that fucking plus sign so bad I thought I'd explode that bathroom, bricks flying from the walls and leaving me sitting on the tiled floor amid rubble and dust and exposed plumbing.

It was positive.

I didn't believe it, so I did another one.

Then I went back to Walgreens and bought two more.

Positive.

Later, when I told my husband he was going to be a dad, he threw both fists in the air home run–style and yelled, "I am captain of the swim team!"

Back at the Golden House, I had a forkful of waffle halfway to my mouth when Dominick's dad got loud. "Are you kidding me? Why do I have to pay for it?" The mom went off next, long strings of sentences filled with obscenities, and across the table my husband raised his eyebrow. It was that uncomfortable moment when you realize you're listening in on someone else's private conversation and probably that's rude, so you try not to, but eventually you just give up. They're too loud—loud and nasty—and after a few minutes the facts become evident: he was emotionally unavailable, she cheated, somebody had to pay the mortgage, who would get the kid, he'd sue her ass in domestic court, she'd love to see him try it, and on and on they went, yelling their heads off but not hearing a thing. You'd think they were speaking different languages: the words came out in English but then got caught in some giant web, so by the time the other one heard what was said, it could've been Greek or Czech or Japanese for all they'd listen, and I shuddered to think that only five minutes before I'd envied them. Dominick started wailing then. Who could blame him? I didn't even know these people and I wanted to cry. "I can't sit here anymore," my husband said, and I nodded—I felt sick, like last month when a whiff of coffee had me running for the toilet. We left some cash on our table, still covered with untouched plates, and went for the door, hands locked together against that couple's yelling and their little boy's crying, and out into the lazy Sunday sun. "I promise," I whispered to my kid. "I promise, I promise, I promise," and my husband squeezed my hand as we crossed the street. I know what it meant—that squeeze. It could've been Greek or Czech or Japanese, but still—I knew.

Logic

Mostly I got a lover 'cause I was lonely, but part of it was I wanted Bobby to stop me. I wanted to see if he'd fight for me, like knights challenging each other to duels all the time. No medieval girls had to wonder if their men loved them, what with everybody swearing everybody's troth all the time, and wearing everybody's pledges in the cuffs of their armor.

I remember the time my dad was docking his fishing boat and me and Mom were walking up the pier to greet him. Some greasy guy in rubber overalls leaned over a pile of rigging and said something to her that started with "little lady," and ended with "whaddya say?" but my eight-year-old vocabulary didn't have time to piece the middle together 'cause Daddy down the dock was already on his feet swinging an industrial shark pole with a fresh-caught hundred-and-twenty-pound halibut over his shoulder. The fish hit the guy square in the face and knocked him flat. It took forever to get the thing disconnected from him 'cause the hook had gone through the halibut's throat and into the guy's eye, and I had to step back from getting blood on my boots. My dad had taken out a guy's eye for even *saying* the wrong thing to my mother, but when I told my husband I was *sleeping* with Eustis Kane he didn't even react. We were on the couch in the living room watching Conan O'Brien and I just busted out with it. "Bobby," I said. "Every night I go to bed with you and you won't touch me." I waited a beat or two, watching his face. It glowed in the blue TV screen light but didn't change, just twitched a couple times and was still. "So," I said, "I found somebody who would touch me in the afternoon."

"Well, isn't that a kick in the teeth?" said Conan.

95

My husband didn't say anything.

I met Bobby a couple Novembers ago, me working at the breakfast place and him coming in on his lunch break. He'd sit there drinking coffee and reading the paper and I'd stand at the far end of the counter, wiping down sticky syrup bottles and staring at him. He was big and bulky, had dark hair, wore thrift-store button-up shirts, chewed on his cuticles. He never said a word to me besides *coffee, sugar,* or *pancakes.* I hadn't had a crush in months and didn't see any other readily accessible options, and since he was cute I let myself fantasize, give him history and personality. After a while, I was damn near crazy about the Him I'd made up.

I'd wait for an excuse to stand near him, monitoring how far back he tipped his head when he drank, and when he'd hit a certain angle I'd refill his coffee cup. By the fourth or fifth the hand holding the newspaper was shaking against the countertop. He never really looked at me though, not even when he mumbled thank you and dropped dollars down. I'd go home and do quizzes in fashion magazines.

> *If your man isn't giving you everything you need, should you:*
> *A. Change him*
> *B. Leave him*
> *C. Find someone else who can.*

Since my man was all in my head, I didn't think it possible that he couldn't deliver everything I needed. When I imagined him, he was perfect.

After a couple months of this behavior I went stark raving crazy and tapped his water glass with a fork to get his attention. "Excuse me," I said. "You see him?" I nodded my head at the guy sitting at the counter eating French toast. "That's Stan. He and his ex-wife are fighting in the courts about who gets to keep their little girl, Dinah. And him," I continued, pointing to the guy at his left with the omelet, "he's on that diet where you only eat eggs and cheese cubes wrapped in bacon. And *that* guy sells fluorescent lighting to big corporate businesses and *that* lady lost her job two weeks back and is always reading the want ads and that kid down at the end is in love with Stella who works here but she thinks he's creepy so she always makes me serve him and it's torture because he just sits there, watching her at her tables, it's enough to break your heart!"

It seems to me that once I start talking I never can find a place to put a period and for that whole time I was babbling away Bobby just stared at his fork-knife-spoon combo and chewed on the inside of his cheek. But there was a second there that he glanced up at me—just a little single second, half a blink even—and I took hold of that and turned it into this huge meaningful victory in my mind so I'd have the guts to keep going.

"My point," I said, setting down the coffeepot and leaning my elbows on the counter, "is that all these people come in here every day and they talk. They tell us everything, like we're hairdressers, and we know all the right questions to ask, like *How's your sick uncle?* or *Did you get the lease on that space?* but we don't know a thing about you. Not your name, not your story, not squat, only that you're in here every day, and friend, the food ain't that good."

The newspaper started shaking then. He'd only had two cups of coffee so it couldn't have been the caffeine. He was looking at the salt and pepper shakers so he wouldn't have to look at me, like maybe there were bugs in the salt and pepper shakers, or gold or something. "I'm Bobby," he said in this super careful voice, and then he grabbed up all his stuff and left in a hurry. *One-two-three* I counted and he came running back in, dropping money on the counter and saying *thankyouverymuch* like it was a single syllable.

I stood there, staring at the space he'd vacated. "What just happened?" I asked. I wasn't asking anyone in particular except maybe God, but all the waitresses I work with took that as their cue to step in and tell me what was what.

"He's shy," said Joan. Joan was eighteen and a virgin.

"You should wear your skirts shorter," said Stella. She was twenty-four and a 36C.

"Crack him over the head," said Elaine. She was twenty-nine and in a hurry.

"Shoot him in the head," said Pearl. Pearl was thirty-three and twice divorced.

"Give it time," said Roberta. Roberta was fifty-four years old and had been married to the same guy for more than half of them. "After I met

Sam," she said, "it took me three years to convince him that he couldn't live another day without me."

So I made a deal with myself to take it one step at a time with Bobby. Every time he came into the restaurant I'd increase the number of words I said to him by one. I'd ease us into each other, sort of like when you quit smoking and you smoke one less—ten a day, nine a day, eight a day—till you're down to nothing.

"Hi," I said, and I filled his coffee cup.

"What's up?" I said the following week while filling his coffee cup.

"How you doing?" I asked politely as I filled his coffee cup.

"What are you reading?" I asked, filling up his cup of coffee.

Somewhere in there I started counting those cups. One cup of coffee, ten cups, twenty, forty, and all he gave me in return were split-second glances and shaky papers. After a while I got frustrated with all the counting on my fingers underneath the counter and decided if he didn't pay attention to me by the time I'd poured his hundredth cup, I was going to throw the goddamn pot at him.

"Seen any good movies lately?" Forty-six cups of coffee.

"How long have you lived here?" Sixty-five cups of coffee.

"Seen any good want ads in there?" Eighty-nine cups of coffee.

"Can you explain this Kuwait business to me?" One fucking hundred.

The coffeepot is glass with an orange plastic decaf handle. It sits sizzling on a burner while slow roast dripdrops into it. I picked it up in my right hand, turned and faced that silent, shaky, beautiful son of a bitch, and flung the pot Frisbee style down the length of the counter. He looked up from his books a spilt second before it hit him full on the side of the face, smashing into his temple and shattering into four solid pieces, boiling coffee exploding and glass slicing into skin.

A couple days later I cashed in a half day's worth of tips and sent an FTD bouquet to the hospital. *Dear Bobby,* said the attached card. *I hope you are doing better. I'm sorry I threw the pot but sometimes you can't control your impulses. Sincerely, your waitress Francine.*

It was a week before I saw him again. He came into the restaurant with a white gauzy eye patch and a purple burn across his cheek, and sat down in his usual spot. I approached him with a cup of coffee and held my breath.

"No girl gave me flowers before," he said. It was the first sentence I ever heard out of his mouth that didn't include nouns indicating breakfast food.

"I'm not like most girls," I said.

"Most girls say that," he said.

I didn't know what to say back. You've got to watch it with those quiet ones, hardly ever open their mouths but when they do it's with something that'll kill you. "I didn't mean to hurt you," I said finally, reaching out for the burn and then pulling my hand away before it got there. "I just wanted you to notice me."

"I always noticed you," he said. Then he smiled.

That, ladies and gentlemen, was the first time I saw my husband smile.

Eventually, things go stale. Bobby'd come home late from work, sneak into bed, and wake up early. He said it was because his construction business was taking off and I needed to be supportive. Then he said I'd have to be patient. Then he said I needed to back off. Even with all those *then he saids*, he never said much. He wasn't what I'd imagined him to be and I was starting to hate him for it, starting to feel more alone with him than I had without him.

So what do you do?

> A. Change him.
> B. Leave him.
> C. Find someone else who can.

I started leaving books by Deepak Chopra around the house and he ignored them. I stayed up till he got home with a list of conversation topics written on the back of my hand and he said he was too tired. I started to wear crazy see-through things and he asked me *What the hell did I have on?* It was after I marched naked into the living room in the middle of the night and yelled, "What do I have to throw at you this time, Bobby?" that he stopped touching me altogether. He'd duck into bed smelling like sawdust and flip over facing the wall. I'd watch his back shiver in sleep, knowing if I didn't find something else to think about, I was going to surge my brain.

99

Eustis Kane is what I found. He was night security at the glass factory and spent his days sitting at my counter, eating eggs and staring at me. I'd never had anybody stare at me like that before. I mean, I'd seen the look, like when my friend Shirley and I would go play pool. We'd walk into the place and some guy'd be bent down over the pool table with his cue lined up on the eight ball, performing some right-angled geometry, and he'd slide the stick through his fingers, giving it a test run or two, and just before he'd let 'er rip he'd be compelled by some higher force—you might say the Lord but I'd wager it was pheromones—to look up and see Shirley. It was all over then, 'cause they'd lock eyes, all hard and penetrating and silksheet grin, eyebrows lifting once, twice, suggesting something, licking lower lip, like a sailor knot tied the two of them together in the electric space between their bodies. So you see, I knew what the look *looked* like, it was just that nobody had ever looked at *me* that way until Eustis Kane started sitting at my counter every day from noon till two-thirty.

I didn't have a good feeling about him. "Weirdo at nine o'clock," I'd tell the other girls, but day after day with somebody shooting that kind of heat in your back, things start burning, let me tell you, and maybe it was so many nights of watching Bobby's back in bed, or maybe it was me running to the ladies every morning at eleven-forty-five to freshen my lipstick, or maybe it was just the simple ease in knowing—absolutely one hundred percent sure—that this here fella wanted me. There wasn't any doubt. No replaying our conversations back over in my head to find where the innuendo was. No eating my liver trying to figure out what the hell he was thinking.

So you could say I was feeling vulnerable on the afternoon Eustis Kane followed me home after work. You could say I was lonely when I nodded my head in the direction of the bedroom. And you could say that I really, really, really needed to get laid when I pulled his belt out of its loops and put my hands on his hips. He's six-foot-five and skinny like a nail, ribs sticking every-which-way out of his chest, his spine poking in hard knuckle-bumps out of his back, every joint sharp and stubbly and pushing skin up and off his body like a windbreaker on a skeleton. We'd lie there, every afternoon from when my shift'd end at three till right before Bobby got home for supper, bedsprings poking up and into my back and pelvic bones poking down and into my front, but it was skin-on-skin and that felt real. The heat was stifling in midday August and sat on us thick like fur, the blankets kicked onto the floor, the fitted sheet skewered sideways from sex gymnastics so my butt was on cotton sheet, and my shoulders were on foam mattress pad, and my legs were in the air.

Afterward, I'd lie with my chin at his armpit, tracing stringy muscles with my fingers, starting high at the knot in his neck and moving down his pointy shoulders: biceps, triceps, wrist, five bumpy rocks topping each finger. *Can I get everything I need from this man?* I'd wonder as I ran my hands along his sides and felt for the crunch hard tips of his ribs, just like you do when you debone a salmon. *Or maybe I could mix the two of them together into one, like how eggs and oil make mayonnaise?* I imagined grabbing Eu's rib bone in my fist and sliding it out of his side like a sword out of its sheath, dropping it to the floor and under the bed. When he'd get up and step into his pants, he'd seem shorter than before. The next day I'd take another one, and he'd have to buckle his belt a couple notches tighter. The day after that he'd be bending forward, curved like some cripple's cane. By the time the whole rack of ribs was hidden under the bed, Eustis Kane would have nothing left to hold him together in the middle and he'd cave right in, just skin and meat and goop. I'd rub him off of me and put the sheets in the wash, and when Bobby would get home from work that night there'd be a pile of bones on a platter on the dining room table.

"Here, baby," I'd say. "Have a spine."

But I didn't say that. I said, "Bobby, I can't keep on sneaking around like this."

He said nothing.

I looked at the burn scar on his cheek and turned back to the television.

The next day, I was acrobatic during and kinda crazy after. Eustis, wiped out from my second orgasm, was lying flat, sleepy and sweating in the August heat. I stood naked on the bed and started jumping up and down, holding my arms out like wings and shutting my eyes so I could pretend I was somewhere else, bouncing on the box spring, up and down like a little girl, electricity buzzing in my middle, shivering, sweating—

"Francie."

I stopped bouncing.

"Francie."

I opened my eyes and Bobby was standing there in the doorway. We stared and I stopped breathing. *Do something!* I thought fiercely, trying to send him my words through my eyes. *Do something!* But he didn't. He turned around and shut the door behind him.

Eustis shocked me out of my shock. "That your husband?" he asked, pulling on his pants.

I gave him that look. That *Are you high?* look.

"Okay," he said. "How much does he weigh?"

Repeat look.

"Not that I can't take him," Eustis went on, zipping, buttoning. "I'd just like to be prepared."

He seemed to interpret my look as need for explanation.

"It's like getting a tetanus shot at the doctor's office, asking if it's gonna hurt," he said. "You're not really scared. You'd just like to know in advance."

I shut my eyes and tried not to scream, which seemed suddenly silly to me so I opened my mouth and screamed as loud as I could, two years' worth of unscreamed scream, seven hundred and thirty stone-still nights counted like coffee cups. I pulled my knees in to my naked chest, curled myself up into a ball, and screamed so long I saw red on the backs of my eyelids, a frozen, suspended moment where everything stopped— Bobby and Eustis and this nagging dissatisfied knot in my stomach—and there was only a high-pitched, scorching sound. It was loud. But not loud enough to block the noise happening outside the bedroom door: scraping on the hardwood floor and banging against the other side of the wall.

I shut my mouth and opened my eyes as Eustis pulled open the bedroom door and ran smack into the back of my china cabinet. It had been in the hallway holding dishes, but now was pushed in front of the door. Bobby must have summoned up that special strength that comes when little kids are trapped under trucks, 'cause that cabinet is heavy maple and it'd taken four guys and a dolly to get it in the house.

Eustis shoved. He turned sideways and leaned his shoulder into it. He turned around and leaned his back into it. He turned around and looked at me. "Uhm," he said, and then there was a bang and the scissorbuzzing of Bobby's drill and before Eustis could get over to the window there was a big stretch of board over it.

"He bought that to reinforce the front porch," I said from the bed, still naked in a ball, and Eustis didn't know what to say.

He tried to say a lot of things during the next few days. He said, "Do you think he'll come back?" and "Are you sure there isn't a phone in here?" and "You got a monopoly board or something?"

After a while he stopped finishing his sentences. He said, "Like you're the first woman who ever—" and "How the hell did I get myself—" and once he flexed his eyebrows and said, "You wanna—" until he caught the look on my face.

"I'll get us out of here, babe," he said, and got a big ol' black-and-blue bruise on his shoulder from banging into the back of the cabinet.

"It's loose now, just one more shove—" he said, and the skin was scraped off his knuckles from punching the windowboard.

I didn't tell him the reason why Bobby's construction business got so busy is 'cause he's really good at it. I didn't say anything at all. I was starting to hate Eustis Kane. I hated him because I'd been wrong about him. He couldn't give me everything.

But maybe there is someone who could. If I get out of this room, I could find him.

Right?

Oscar and Veronica

They were always together, talking about how alone they were. They'd be in the lounge area of the Lennox Hotel, sitting on plushy couches, waiting for the waitress to bring them drinks.

"I'm scared it's always going to be this way," she'd say, her voice melancholy.

"I know," he'd say. He'd look around to see if anyone was listening, and then lean in close and whisper, "And I'm almost thirty."

"Yes," she'd say, "but you're a guy. You're fortunate. Women sag sooner." She'd poke herself in the stomach, indicating the layer of baby fat that she couldn't yoga off. He'd gasp, very *I can't believe you just said that!*, and pull on the loose skin under his neck. She'd grab the dangle of her upper arm, and he'd take a fistful of lovehandle at his side. They were two attractive people who felt self-conscious about stupid things, and saw no problem wasting hours in this silly one-uppance. Sometimes, though, they'd agree with each other. They'd lean back in the couch, arms linked, silly from the rum in their frothy drinks saying *I know, I know, I know.*

"I just don't know how to approach someone."

"I know!"

"Everybody makes it sound so easy, so *hi there, you're perfect.*"

"I know! I wish someone would do that to me!"

"I know! Me TOO!"

They used great detail, like this:

"I'm getting desperate. I fall for men that are bad for me. Men who drink too much. Men who have girlfriends. Men who aren't honest, like if I kiss them in the corner, the next time I see them we have to pretend like it never happened." He nodded, absently. He'd heard this one before, and wiggled his butt down into the couch cushions, looking for the perfect spot. "And have you noticed," she continued, oblivious, "all of them have tattoos? Like the guy with the Vonnegut tattoo. I think the only reason why I went out with him is because I loved that book. When, in all truth—"

He cut her off. He'd already listened to what he thought was a fair share of Guy with the Vonnegut Tattoo stories. "How about me?" he said. "At least you're kissing guys. At least they're falling for you. You've got options. When you get the look, you know it's—"

"What look?"

"You know, THE look."

"No, I don't know. Look at me with it."

They sat up straight and turned toward each other. He looked at her very intensely, right in the eyes. Usually, when people look, they look at the bridge of the other person's nose, or maybe the middle of their forehead. Right in the eyes was a hard business. It was more like right in the *eye*, because you focus on one very specific place, one eye, one pupil, one iris in the pupil. You look so hard, if somebody'd ask you afterward what color the eyes were of the person you were looking at, you wouldn't know. Your concentration would be so deep you wouldn't have the effort left to remember what you saw.

He knew what color her eyes were, though. Green. He'd been looking at them for five years almost.

After a beat or two, he looked away.

"You looked away," she pointed out. She wrapped a strand of hair around one finger and started tugging.

"I looked away *after* I looked," he said. "After I transmitted information." He put one arm over the back of the couch and leaned back, pleased with himself.

She leaned into his arm. "What information?"

"Any information. Like, with you, if I've been telling you for weeks about the guy with the funny nose, and then we're at a party and I'm talking to the guy with the funny nose, and I look at you, and look at him, and back at you, I've just transmitted information. The *this is the guy I've been talking about* information. Whereas if I'm out at the bars, and some guy is looking at me, and I look at him, then we're transmitting information, too, but a different kind."

She found this analogy strange because he never went to the bars. *The* capitalized, T-H-E bars, the gay bars. She thought he didn't go because he hated them, when in reality he was just scared to go alone and didn't want to tell her, because, probably, she'd offer to come, and what would happen then? Something growled in her gut that she should leave all this alone, and asked, instead, "What different kind of look?"

"See, that's what I'm saying!" He was very excited. He sloshed some of his drink as he set it down on the low table in front of their couch. He needed to use his arms to answer this question. "If *you* look at a guy and he looks at you, the information you've exchanged is *hi there, hi, you're cute, so are you, is it on? it's on!* whereas with me, I've got to go through all the *are you gay or not, or friendly or not, or attracted or not, or available or not, or is it okay that I'm even looking at you or not* before I can even begin exchanging the *it's on!* information!" He slumped back into the couch, exhausted. "You can never totally tell. It's all fifty-fifty. Or actually, more like twenty-eighty, whatever the gay to straight statistic is nowadays. Do you know what it is nowadays?"

She didn't. But she knew he was hurting so she took his hand and stroked it, and he put his arm around her again. They slurped their rum and felt sorry for themselves.

Sometimes, they needed to take a break from feeling sorry for themselves. When they did, they played a game: she would sit with her back to the room, and he would face it. He would tell her what was happening behind her, and she had to guess if it was true or not. She could ask any questions she wanted, but she couldn't turn around. One time, they were at El Chino on Milwaukee Avenue, drinking frozen margaritas out of plastic goblets. "Oh my gosh!" he said, staring over her shoulder and out the front window. "I can't believe it!"

Instinct would have you turn around in a moment such as this, but she knew better. "What is it?" she asked, resisting the temptation and looking at him instead, and he spun a crazy story about the jeep parked out front, and how someone had just broken into it, the wild police chase that ensued, and the whole time she just stared into his face, knowing everything she needed was right there.

Then the break was over. Time to get back to it.

"I'm so alone."

"Me too."

"I'll never meet anyone."

One day, he said, "We'll never meet anyone *here*." He swung his eyes around the interior of the Lennox: High ceilings. Gilded windows with heavy drapes. Waitresses in tuxedo vests and short skirts. Businessmen with expensive ties loosened at their throats, sprawled on soft couches, drinking brandy or coffee, talking in very loud voices about things that should be immediately followed by a cymbal crash. "The kind of people we want to be with are not here."

She asked, very seriously, "What kind of people do we want to be with?"

They thought of some adjectives: Honest. Creative. Intelligent. Fun. Comfortable.

"Comfortable?" he said. "Comfortable like how?"

"Comfortable like this," she said. She waved her hand around in the empty space between them. "I want it to be as easy as this." She got a little worked up as she spoke, tears in her eyes and whatnot.

He patted her hand. "This didn't happen overnight," he said. "We've known each other a long time."

They had. They'd gone to graduate school in the city and had a night class together. Upon dismissing class the first day, the instructor made everybody buddy-up on the El, safety in numbers and all, and they'd discovered they lived in the same neighborhood. The walk to the station was delightful: dark sky, gentle winter night, good conversation, the excitement of possibility. She'd just gotten away from yet another tattooed guy who was bad for her—one who drank too much, who had a girlfriend, who wasn't honest—and was caught in that uncomfortable place between being distrustful with men and lonely without them. After a pleasant half hour of Not Lonely, she made a snap decision about which feeling was worse, and summoned all her courage.

"Do you want to have dinner with me?" she said, and then turned her face away as though anticipating a blow. This was the first time she'd ever asked a man out on a date. She was from a small Midwestern town and had been brought up very old-school, very he holds the door open, he comes in to meet the parents, he makes the requisite phone call. But five years of liberal education—essays by Adrienne Rich, press conferences about Anita Hill, dormitories full of post–Gloria Steinem girls who spoke out loud about equality and in secret waited by their telephones—well, it had all confused the issue, for better or worse, and she crossed her fingers in her mittens. What would he say, what would he say?

"Sure," he said.

Hooray!

And then: "I mean, I'm gay. But I'd love to have dinner with you."

Shall we talk a little more about confusing the issue?

"Where do we go to meet people?" he wondered. Then: "Where did *we* meet?" He had no memory of such details; rarely do you remember everything about the first time you met a friend. She on the other hand, if pressed, could tell you about the orange waffle sweater he'd been wearing. She could tell you about how heavy his backpack seemed from all the books he carried, and the way the streetlight lit up the sidewalk, that he held the door open for her, and, after most of the things she'd said, he'd said, *I know!*

"Not anyplace like here," she said. She looked around the lounge. It was so fancy, with big chandeliers, thick carpet, and little flipbooks on the tables with all the drinks listed. No prices, though. Much too fancy for that. But with all the glitz came a certain sterility, like when you go to a place every day but are still never quite comfortable in it.

"Where then?" he asked. He was frustrated. "Like, people are always telling you to play the field, but they never tell you where it is! If I knew where it was, I'd go there! I'd pack a lunch!"

They asked the waitress for a pen, and on the back of a bar napkin they made a list. On the top of it they wrote: *Fields*. Underneath that, they wrote:

Bar (new ones)
Beach
Bikram class
Waiting rooms (doctor/dentist)
Foot Locker (?)

Bookstore
Whole Foods
Dinner parties (hosted by single people)

In the following weeks, they went everywhere on their list. Together.

They sat at bars with their heads together. They put sunblock on each other's backs. They put their yoga mats side-by-side and exhaled nam. They waited. They sampled cheese and different hummus flavors, and all throughout, they never met the kind of people they'd want to be with, not until her sister Phyllis had a dinner party and promised loads of single men. "Loads," they'd gloated over the phone the night before. "Loads!"

She arrived first, and kept herself busy chopping cauliflower for the veggie dip plate. Three different men approached her as she chopped and asked if she needed help. "I mean, how many people do you need to chop a cauliflower?" she asked once he got there, breathless out of the night. "Seems to me you're doing a fine job on your own," he said, pouring her wine. Nobody approached either one of them again until she went off to the bathroom, and a tall guy in a polo shirt came up and said hello to him. He said hello back, and then they talked about other things until she returned. "I'm back!" she announced, running into the kitchen, wrapping her arms around him from behind. The polo shirt looked her up and down and left. She chatted away, not noticing that he was watching the empty hallway that the polo shirt had just disappeared down. Eventually, he looked back at her and asked, "Do you think—" and stopped.

"What?" she asked.

"It's too silly," he said.

"Tell me," she insisted.

"Do you think people never approach us because they think that we're . . . together?"

"No!" she exclaimed, then wrinkled her eyebrows as if she wasn't quite sure.

They had to realize it eventually, I mean, come on. They're smart, well-educated people. It was just a matter of time.

So they devised a plan. It was called Oscar and Veronica and it worked like this: if either one saw a man they were attracted to, they would start calling one another Oscar or Veronica. This was the signal that they were brother and sister, and should immediately begin talking about brother-sister things as loudly as possible, while still seeming nonchalant. That was the trick.

"Did Mom call?"

"I'm going to visit Grandma next week."

"Dad just infuriates me!"

These were all acceptable lines of dialogue in the Oscar and Veronica game, and they had a great deal of fun practicing. So much fun, in fact, that it was months and months before they ever got around to *using* it.

When they finally did, it happened like this:

They were drinking cappuccinos at a place in the Gold Coast. They'd added Gold Coast to their list, right there under dinner parties, thinking that maybe the kind of people they wanted to be with were grown-ups, and maybe grown-up meant financially secure, and financially secure meant Gold Coast.

She stood at the counter, adding milk to her coffee, when she heard it: "Hey, Veronica. Can you grab me some sugar?"

She turned back to the table where Oscar sat waiting. It was small, only two people could fit, and next to it was another small table with a guy. A very good-looking guy, but not so good-looking he was intimidating. He was Not Good-Looking enough to still take home to your parents. You could spill milk on your shirt in front of him. He was real, in a nice blue sweater and nice Jack Spade bag and nice MacBook Pro set up on the table which he was very busy not looking at because he was busy looking at Oscar.

Veronica felt a little kick in her chest. Then she went to the table, sitting down with her back to the guy, facing Oscar, who had a look on his face that she'd never seen before.

It was a look that transmitted information.

"Did you talk to Mom?" he said, loudly, but not too loud. It was a small coffee shop; his voice would travel to the table behind them. Veronica saw that he wasn't really looking at her—he was looking at the space just to the side of her. He was looking past her, and he was smiling. When did smiling become part of this? Had the transmission been accepted? What was happening? She longed to turn around but knew that wasn't part of the game. The game was staring straight ahead and saying, loud enough, "I did talk to her. She asked if you were coming for Christmas."

He smiled again, but this time—the first time—not for her.

She had to realize it eventually, I mean, come on. She's a smart girl. It was just a matter of time.

All So Goddamn Great

So I'm at the Metro for the EXO show and it—is—*awesome.* There are like five million people all suctioned together, banging our heads in unison like we're part of some collective unconscious and me and my friend Betsy are right up near the front so we can feel the speakers vibrate through our shoes. I'm wearing my EXO T-shirt 'cause EXO is totally the greatest band like ever and if you say, *No they're not,* I'll be all, *You don't know what the hell you're talking about,* 'cause I'm twenty-two-years old and totally smarter than everyone.

It's one of those nights, you know, when everything is *just . . . so . . . great!* The music is great, this vodka tonic is great, this other vodka tonic is great, and so's this other one, and for the first time since Josh and I broke up last month, I know I'll be okay. Strangers press into me on all four sides, I'm slamming both fists in the air, there's guitar and bass and dududududududududu and I yell *Hell yeah!* and Betsy's like *This is awesome!* and I'm like *I gotta pee!* and she's like *Fuck yeah you do!*

And then we hug.

'Cause it's all so goddamn great!

I do the drunky wobble-walk, pushing though the crowd and then upstairs toward the bathroom, hand-over-hand on the banister 'cause I've got heels on, and falling down the stairs is so not cool, so I focus like how I learned in yoga class: *one foot, then the other, then the other, you're doing great,* and when I finally get to the top I throw my arms in the air and look around for applause, like *I just totally made it up the stairs without falling over I'm so awesome!* and then I look up and there's Josh.

He looks good.

He's super tall and skinny—but not like skinny-skinny, like muscle-skinny—with the whole bad-boy thing going on. That's what hooked me: night after night, sittin' in some bar with his arm around me, and he's all *Yeah, she's with me,* and I'm all *I'm with him I'm with him I'm with him!* so yes, seeing him really sucks, but what sucks more is that now he's got his arm around some other girl.

Some other beautiful girl.

Some other beautiful girl who's twenty pounds thinner than me and obviously much cooler 'cause she's wearing sunglasses in a darkened rock club and also she's got perfect, silky, shiny hair like *Don't hate me because I'm beautiful. My hair used to have a mind of its own, but then I started using Pantene*—that hair. On *this* girl. Josh's girl, she's here with Josh, they're leaning against the upstairs bar and haven't seen me yet, which would be so *totally* too much for me to handle, so, I split—I leave—I turn—I run to the ladies' room, the only place we're ever really safe.

The one at the Metro is this long narrow room with stalls against one wall and a sink at the very end. There's a thin layer of *What in the hell even is that?* over everything, and bright fluorescent lights which are total buzzkill. Plus there's never any toilet paper, and the stalls all have those graffiti conversations that go *Lisa plus Johnny forever,* and underneath that somebody else wrote *There is no forever, only heartbreak* and underneath that somebody else wrote *Shut up* and underneath that somebody wrote the letter U, the letter R, the letter A—*bitch* and this is what I stare at while I cry; that sloppy gaspy gulpy crying, the kind where you can't control the corners of your mouth, which is so totally stupid because I don't even want to be with Josh.

I don't.

The last time I saw him was a month ago, this horrible, fuzzy night at Inner Town Pub. One second it was just like always: we were drinking, laughing, feeding quarters to the jukebox—then the next second some guy asked if he could buy me a beer and before I had time to say *No thanks, I'm with him*—it was the next second and *bam*—Josh slammed the guy into the bar, yelling *You asshole!* and I was like *Josh, he didn't know*—but the guy shoved back, so then Josh was on the floor, and then he was up again, and then he had his stool over his head and before anyone could stop him he threw it over the bar and into the mirrored wall behind it.

I remember watching the multiple reflections of shocked faces as slowly, slowly, the glass spiderwebbed, like how water cracks through the walls of a sunken ship. It took approximately ten seconds for the bouncer to tackle him, but during those ten seconds, Josh went after me.

Ten seconds is a really long time.

I remember him reaching for me, I remember the veins in his arms, purple rivers on a map, his biceps like baseballs, and people were on their feet now, backing away from us, and I backed away from him coming at me, and he was yelling and I was confused 'cause apparently this was my fault? I'd said/worn/done/thought/felt the wrong thing, but I didn't have time to piece it all together because there were his hands reaching for my face, but just before they connected, the bouncer caught him from behind, his meatball arms locking around Josh's neck and—

I was lucky.

The next morning, he called. I didn't pick up. "I've got a bitch of a hangover," he told my voicemail. "Must've been a crazy night!"

"What's up?" he said the next day. "How come you're not calling back?"

"Dude, what the hell," he said on the third day, and, "What's the matter with you?" on the fourth, and by the end of the week it was, "Baby, are you okay?" and "Did something happen?"

Yeah. Something did. I was different: no more light and naive and free. Now I had baggage, a big heavy suitcase to carry from relationship to relationship, and the worst of it was—the part that really makes me hate myself?—I wanted to pick up that phone. I wanted to believe in him, to say *He was tired drunk, he was drunk, he was stressed out* because sometimes? When you're twenty-two? Being with somebody bad for you is better than being alone—and believe me, you're never more alone than sitting in a bathroom stall, crying your eyes out 'cause your boyfriend found someone else.

I stay in that stall for a really long time, listening to EXO through the walls, but it's not near loud enough to make everything okay. I'm sweaty and wasted and sloppy, there's snot everywhere, mascara all over my face, this isn't fun drunk anymore, it's stupid drunk, and once I'm cried out I head to the sink to try and clean up, but when I round the corner of the stalls, the thing I see next makes me so totally sober I could've walked straight across a tightrope.

114

It's her, standing in front of the mirror with her back to me: twenty pounds thinner, long Pantene hair—we're so close that if I had a pair of scissors in my pocket I could reach out and cut it off and, yes, I know, what you're supposed to do in these moments is turn around and walk away—but I don't, 'cause you never do, you always, always, always *stare*. Her sunglasses are on the sink in front of her, she's looking down into an open makeup bag, and in the mirror over her shoulder I see that both her eyes are black.

The bruises are caked with cover-up, but those horrible fluorescent lights forgive nothing: her eyes are two goose eggs, purple-black and nearly swollen shut. The slits of her eyes are bloodshot, but if it's from crying or drinking I can't say. The bruises run up to her brows and down past her cheekbones; they are painful and brutal and fascinating, a car crash, a science experiment, I can't look away—not even when she looks up and sees me in the mirror, my reflection just behind hers.

For years afterward, well into my thirties, I will imagine our faces switched: me with the black eyes and her staring from behind. I will imagine what might've happened if that bouncer hadn't caught Josh in a headlock, if his outstretched hands had reached my face, and how much heavier my baggage would be. I will imagine, when I shut my eyes, a bullet flying straight for the center of my forehead—and how, at the last possible second, I stepped to the side and dodged its impact, and I will imagine, again and again, what I should have said to that girl in the bathroom 'cause in the moment? Standing next to her at the sink? I had absolutely no idea.

I am twenty-two years old. I am terrified. So I say nothing.

I look away, like I didn't see anything, and she looks away, like there was nothing there to see.

And then I leave.

Out in the hall, it's a different world: dark, and safe, the music's full volume and it pounds into my chest. I'm part of the crowd again, no more me all by myself, now there are bodies, five hundred faces to hide behind. I follow some random girl toward the stairs, staring at the back of her head, the back of her head, the back of her head, 'cause if I look up, even for a second, there's a chance I might see Josh—and I've had enough of him for one night.

Once I'm on the main floor, I push through the bodies toward where I left Betsy, up by the speakers where not ten minutes before everything had seemed so easy: music and dancing and people and vodka, it's all so goddamn great! Betsy's jumping up and down, punching the air with both fists, and when she sees me she yells *There you are!*

Yeah, I say, but she's not listening. *I'm gonna get another drink do you want another drink?* she yells, and even though my head's starting to hurt, even though strangers are slamming into me, even though my life just entirely changed—I still say *Yeah, sure I'll have another*, because I don't know what else to do with this stupid, stupid night or my stupid, stupid heart—so I shut my eyes. I feel the music vibrate through my shoes, and—I dance.

Indestructible

When I was a kid, my dad took me to New York City. For "culture."
We did the usual—museums, Times Square, Forty-Second Street—and
the day before we left was Coney Island. It was August, hot as hell. I'm in
pigtails and an OshKosh jumper, and my dad's got white legs under his
shorts and a sunburnt bald spot. He bought Big Gulp–sized Coca-Colas
from a vendor, and I scooped the ice and rubbed it on my arms to cool
off. There weren't a lot of people out that day, and we went up and down
the boardwalk looking at the water, the old decaying roller coasters, and
the freak-show booths with their colorful circus posters promising sword
swallowers and contortionists. My dad paid the buck fifty so we could go
into a couple: inside they were small and claustrophobic like the dressing
rooms at JC Penney, except when you pulled back the curtain there was
some funky-looking person standing there.

Like, *ta-da!* The Fat Lady!

Ta-da! The Albino Midget!

Ta-da! Siamese Twins!

But none of this was particularly impressive to my seven-year-old sen-
sibility 'cause I'd seen *way* fatter women at the airport, and Ms. Astors,
the librarian at my school, was a "little person," and I could tell that the
twins weren't *really* joined 'cause I saw that the one on the left had his
extra arm turned up behind his back.

But then—*ta-da!* Hold onto your hats, boys and girls, for what you are
about to see scoffs in the face of science, defies every rule of anatomy, and
busts open Darwinian theory by its sheer impossibility: *The Indestructible
Lady!*

The curtain was thrown aside, and my jaw must've hit the ground. I had to tilt my head back, back, back, till I was almost looking at the ceiling. BIG. She. Was. BIG. That's all I would've been able to tell you then, but looking back on her now I can do the description justice. She was way over six feet with that male professional bodybuilder body you see in the Mr. Universe pageants: big hulking muscles that pushed at her thighs and six-packed her stomach. She was wearing a little red string bikini but she didn't need the top—the cut of her pecs buried any breasts she might once have had. Her neck was as wide as her waist, and her arms popped with softball bulges at the shoulders, triceps, and right above the inside of her elbows. She curled her arms at L-shaped angles and the muscles jumped. She tensed her legs and, I swear, you could trickle water through the definition of her quads.

What got me, though, were the knives. This lady had knives stuck through her skin, big long knives like Dad used to skin deer in the garage back home in Michigan. They had fancy hilts with fake jewels, and they spliced through one side of the Indestructible Lady's arm or leg and came out the other. I tried to count them . . . one, two, twelve, twenty, twenty-two. Twenty-*two* knives cutting into this woman *right* in front of me—no blood, no pain, just clenched teeth, curled upper lip, and every now and then she growled.

"Daddy," I said, as we left the booth. "That's what I want to be when I grow up."

"What?" he asked.

"Indestructible," I said.

We killed a few more hours on the boardwalk and were getting ready to go back to the hotel when all the Coca-Cola caught up with me. I was a little girl, and Big Gulps are a lot of soda, and when I ran over to the door that said Ladies, it was locked. I clenched hard and waited—waited and waited and waited—for whoever was in there to finish. I stuck both hands between my legs and squeezed—I made the squeeze face, eyes all squinted, mouth pulled up, nose tight till my eyeballs hurt, and finally I couldn't hold it anymore so I knocked, and—get this: The door opened and there were the thighs. The red bikini bottoms, sparse as dental floss. The stomach. The chest. The hulky, hammy neck. The knives still splitting her flesh, in and out like a pin through your pant leg, and when my head was bent back as far as it could go I was looking right into the Indestructible Lady's face.

She was crying.

Her skin was swollen and puffy and her mouth was twitching at the sides, like when you're trying to control it but can't. The whites of her eyes were red and veiny and full of water, and it was horrible, and fascinating, and I couldn't look away.

"What are you staring at?" she asked finally.

I was so starstruck, I couldn't even speak.

"Well?" she said.

I tried to be brave. "Is it the knives?" I asked, in not more than a whisper.

"Is it the knives what?" she said.

"That make you cry," I said.

She stared at me from her impossible height. Then, slowly, she knelt down until we were eye level, so close our noses were almost touching. "The knives?" she said, and tapped the hilt stuck deep in the meat of her shoulder. "Sweetheart, the knives ain't nothing."

Everyone Remain Calm

You know the drill. There's this long, droning horn and that means tornado. The teacher tells everybody to *Remain calm, this is just a drill,* and your second grade class stands up in unison and lines up alphabetically at the door. What happens next is you walk out to the hall in an orderly fashion and stand with your back up against the lockers. Then you slide down to the floor, tuck your head into your knees, and put your hands over your neck. *This is to prevent paralysis in case anything falls on you,* you are told. When you ask what will be falling, you are told flying debris. When you ask what "debris" means, you are told to *Shhhh, be quiet, you must pretend this is a real tornado. This is real danger. During real danger, no one must talk.* But everybody knows the tornado drill is just practice danger, so everybody goofs off. They poke the kid next to them. Make jokes. Laugh.

Nobody did that the day there was a real tornado, though.

The wind was loud outside and everyone was scared, lined up in the halls, squeezed into balls with their hands over the backs of their necks and their eyes shut tight. The wind screeched—rattled the building—and I could feel the lockers quivering at my back, shaking against the base of my spine and with every bam-blast there were gasps and screams and cries from little kids all terrified. Ms. Atkins was yelling *Everyone must remain calm, this is just a drill,* and then there was an awful noise and I peeked up between my elbows. The windows had busted through, glass was everywhere, wind was whipping all around, and suddenly I learned what debris was—papers, book bags, rain hats, rolling garbage cans, all the red and yellow construction-paper fish the third graders had made for a bulletin board about the ocean, crayons and open tubes of glitter and banners with the cursive alphabet, all of it flying, whirling around in the air past my nose—it's magic, I thought—but then Ms. Atkins was screaming *Everyone remain calm* and she sure-as-shooting didn't look calm. Her hair was all flyaway around her head like she had one hand on a balloon and she was holding tight to a door, the wind lifting her up off the ground, yelling *This is just a drill, it's pretend*, and I thought I would blow away, too. Then Jimmy Azrial, who sat alphabetically next to me, grabbed hold of my arm with his left hand, keeping his right on the back of his neck. I grabbed hold of Elisabeth Benning the same way, and she grabbed hold of Kyle Burns, and so on down the line till we were one long chain of little bodies up against the lockers, our collective weight holding us down. I pressed my eyes into my knees and whispered over and over *It's just pretend, pretend, pretend*, and later when I went home and it wasn't there anymore, just a big ol' pile of boards and splinters and tossed-around furniture, I looked up at my father and said, "I thought it was pretend."

He didn't say anything back, because he was trying to figure out how to tell me that my mother had been in that house when the tornado hit and now—she wasn't.

It got worse. My first year in college I fell asleep studying with the window open, and a storm started up while I slept. The wind blew into my room and suddenly I could see her, green dress, yellow hair, the image from a photograph animated in my mind, her in the house during the tornado, running through rooms, grabbing onto anything stationary—the bed, the banister, the closet doors. Everything she got her hands around was ripped away from her, spiraling up and into the funnel of wind that sucked up the couch and the cabinets and the walls and her, too, all of it flying debris spinning clockwise to the sky like a drain in reverse. The wind shook my dorm room and I woke up on the floor, knees pulled to my chest, head tucked to my knees, hands locked over the back of my neck, shaking, squeezing—

"Breathe," says Earl. "Breathe." He rubs my back until the shaking stops, until I am quiet. "Just breathe."

Earl is my boyfriend. I know. I don't get it either—why he stays. None of the rest of them did. I'd go out with guys in college, and we'd sit there at the bar-restaurant-library-bookstore-club-quad-theater-coffeeshop having the first-date conversation. You know the one I mean, where you ask subtle questions in order to figure out what's wrong with one another. You say things like *Do you want to have kids someday?* or *Tell me about your past relationships* or *Have you ever been incarcerated?* And they say things like *No, the world is too overpopulated* or *We just broke up* or *Yes, but I'm completely rehabilitated now.* You ask the questions and you get the answers, it's expected. But nobody ever expects me to lean back in my chair, cross my arms in front of my chest, and say, dead serious, deadpan, "I'm an amenophobiac."

There is a long pause. Then they panic, because they don't know what amenophobia means and they are imagining crazy things, like maybe I am afraid of . . . I don't know, *chins*. Or *sitting*. There were all sorts of triggers in my phobia support group. People afraid of pleasure. Moisture. Stars. Small things. The color yellow, bears, beef, running water, loud noises, whirlpools, loneliness; being stared at, looked at, talked to; ithyphallophobia (seeing, thinking about, or having an erect penis); chiraptophobia (being touched); deipnophobia (dinner conversation); or philophobia (falling in love). So when they say, "What's amenophobia?" there is caution in their voice.

"It's the fear of wind," I say, and they study me, trying to ascertain whether or not I am serious, decide I must be joking, and burst into laughter. "Ha ha," they laugh. "That was a good one. You sure are a witty girl."

If I'm feeling kind, I simply ask for the check and leave. But usually, I enjoy finding a scapegoat. "How *dare* you laugh," I say, bitterly, and continue with a scorching lecture about tolerance toward the psychologically challenged.

I didn't have a lot of second dates.

Earl was different, though. When I told Earl I had amenophobia, he said, "Okay. Do you want to get a bottle or just order by the glass?"

Perhaps he needed clarification. "I am afraid of wind," I said, careful to enunciate.

He looked around the restaurant. "You think it's windy in here?" he asked.

I sat quietly for a moment and felt—all still. "No," I said.

122

He set the wine list down and looked at me. "Dating is hard enough as is," he said. "Let's just cross bridges when we come to them."

We came to it a couple weeks later, on the fourth date. We were doing one of those hand-in-hand walks by the lake at twilight kind of things, and I was trying to figure out how I got so lucky while simultaneously holding up my end of the conversation. That's when I felt it, on the side of my face. I tried to inhale like my yoga instructor taught me, tried to find my calm, *You must remain calm*, but my heart was pounding and that pounding moved up into my head and down to my toes. I gripped Earl's hand tighter and tighter till he said "Uhm, ow, that hurts," and I said "We're coming to the bridge, Earl!" and shut my eyes tight, like a little kid covering her face during hide-and-seek—if I can't see it, it can't get me—but it can, it is, it's here, it's cold, I can't, I'm scared—"

"Breathe," Earl said. "Just breathe."

That's what he always says.

One time, he tried to say something else. He said: "This is all in your head." We were in Wilderness Outfitters and I was trying to special-order a full-body jumpsuit made out of wind resistant fabric. "I have a medical condition," I said to the salesgirl, who insisted they didn't manufacture such suits. "If I was in a wheelchair, would you tell me they didn't make ramps?" Earl grabbed hold of my arm, excused us for a moment, and walked me to the front door.

He said it then: "This is all in your head."

I didn't react very well to that observation. "Fuck you," I said. "Fuck you, fuck you, fuck you, it is not all in my head." I pushed open the door and walked outside. It was April in Chicago—storm season—and the sky was heavy, gray; in a few hours it would explode, a faucet from above, but in the meantime the wind tackled me like a football player and I tilted almost diagonal as I pushed back against it. In my chest, I felt the panic, couldn't breathe, like someone tied knots around my trachea, but I had something to prove to Earl and everyone. In my pockets, I found some scraps of paper and let the wind take them. They whipped through the air and I hurried back inside. "You see that?" I asked. My breath came in punches. "That's reality if I ever saw it."

Earl sighed—he'd been doing that a lot lately. "Okay. Wind is real, but the fear of it—"

"There *is* reason to fear it," I said, my words all cold. "I know there is, I know!" I went on with all the statistics I'd collected over the years, people who'd lost their lives in the wind, lost homes and towns and all sorts of catastrophe. I threw the numbers at him like bullets; it wasn't just my mother, it had been a lot of people, I mean, in the Midwest alone—

"Okay," he said. "Fine."

Usually, he fought me. He'd say stuff you read in self-help books, how there's more to life than fear—but there's only so long you can talk when you know nobody hears it.

I didn't hear it. I heard meteorology reports on wind patterns, websites on natural disasters, pain on the news; and then saw the world through a thin line of vision between the scarf wrapped around my face and the scarf wrapped around my head. I never left the house without completely wrapping up. Eventually, I never left the house at all.

But the thing is—it gets in.

I am sitting on the floor, in the doorway between my bedroom and the hall. My back is pressed up against the frame, my knees are pulled into my chest, my head is tucked into my knees, my hands are locked over the back of my neck to protect my spine. The wind is howling something awful and the rain is beating on the roof, my heart is thumpkicking against my chest and I jolt with every thunderbolt. I wonder if this is what she felt—this panic—this fear—this screaming in her stomach as the house whipped up around her, furniture and floorboards flying to the sky and did she put her hands over the back of her neck? Did she grab hold of the door frame? Did she remain calm? Because I really need to know what to do here, I need to know what to—

"Breathe," Earl yells over the roar of the wind. "Just breathe." He is running all around the apartment closing windows, and I can feel the air calm around me—except for the left side. I can still feel it on the left side, and the knots around my windpipe constrict. I gasp for air and peek out over my elbows—a window is stuck. Earl is trying to push it down. He jabs at it with the meat of his palm, sinks his weight into it, nothing. The wind is getting in.

But in that last, fragile second before I lose control, I see a single paper streamer caught in the breeze. It's yellow, left over from a birthday party last week, and it does a little dance in the wind. It dips and twists and swirls in front of me, and I remember the moment when I thought this was magic. And once I've started looking, I see other things, too, like the books on the shelf that I've never read, and the wine on the counter I've never tasted, and Earl standing by the window who maybe I could love.

I just have to get up.

ACKNOWLEDGMENTS

My profound gratitude to Parneshia Jones for believing in this book and giving it a new life, and to the team at Northwestern University Press for their fierce care of my ten-years-ago heart, especially my editor Anne Gendler for the conversations in the margins. My agent, Meredith Kaffel Simonoff, is an angel from somewhere on high; thank you for advocating for my past work as lovingly as you do my future.

When I was a kid, my dad told me stories and my mom read books to me. They've given me many gifts over the years, but I'm most grateful for those stories and books. If I can be half the parent they are, my son is lucky.

Thank you to the audience, staff, and storytellers of 2nd Story who've inspired and challenged me for two decades, and the countless writing students I've worked with who put their hearts on the page and hand those pages to me. Your stories made me who I am: writer, teacher, parent, citizen, human being on this planet.

Thank you to the Black Mountain Institute, where I dug back into these pages and wrestled with my past. The support of this organization came at a critical time in my life when I needed reminding that my work has value and I should keep going.

Your work has value. Keep going.

Thank you to Derrick Robles and John Latino at the Bongo Room, whose friendship and business supported me while I figured out what the hell I was doing. I hope every young artist finds a place like this, with good work that pays your rent and good people who love you always.

All of this—the working and the writing and the living—takes a village. Lucky for me, I have one. The best one. Thank you to Randy Albers, Dia Penning and Jess Tschirki, Sarah and Scott Zematis, Samantha Irby and Kirsten Jennings, Beth and Jeff Scales, Amanda Delheimer, Khanisha Foster, Lott Hill, Kristin Lewis, Molly Each, and my dear Jeff Oaks. Again and again, you told me I could do it. Again and again, you told me I could do it better.

My whole heart is for Caleb Jobson, who was three years old when this book first came out and thirteen while I edited the new edition. We lived in four states that year, on the road during a global pandemic with two laptops, for remote teaching and remote seventh grade, and one night in the kitchen in California he asked what I was doing. "I'm rewriting my first book," I told him.

"I bet you changed a lot," he said. "Would you change anything in the writing?"

"No," I said. "Everything here brought me to you."